Philip

A Novel

Philip
A Novel

Chris Duffett

GILEAD
B O O K S
PUBLISHING

First published in Great Britain, November 2017

www.GileadBooksPublishing.com

2 4 6 8 10 9 7 5 3 1

Copyright © Chris Duffett 2017

British Library Cataloguing-in-Publication Data:

A catalogue record for this book is available from the British Library.

ISBN: 978-1-9997224-1-8

The scripture quotation on page 140 (Psalm 96:1-6) is taken from GOD'S WORD®, © 1995 God's Word to the Nations. Used by permission of Baker Publishing Group.

The scripture quotation on page 237 (Isaiah 53:3-6) is from the New Revised Standard Version Bible, copyright 1989, Division of Christian Education of the National Council of the Churches of Christ in the United States of America. Used by permission. All rights reserved.

Dedicated to...

Two modern-day and very-much-alive Philips who have inspired me to keep doing what I do.

Firstly, Jon Philips. You were the very first person I had the joy of properly trying to help grow as a follower of Jesus, and to see what you do now just blows me away. You help me stay close to Jesus. The student has truly become the teacher.

Secondly, Phillipe Gatti. Of all the people I've ever known, you live the life like Philip the evangelist the most. Your adventures day by day and your long journeys around the world with Veronique are an inspiration to me.

And also to one Philip who has died. The very original one who has gone to be with Jesus; the one and only evangelist Philip. The way you met and showed the love of God to that eunuch has carried on inspiring me as I meet all kinds of people. Because of you, rather than being repelled by their differences I have experienced the love the Father has for them, and I see His beauty within them. Your story has become my story. Thank you for your obedience to go and reach out to those who were considered beyond the fringe of salvation. I hope that this book makes you smile and that we can grab a coffee and talk about it one day in the mystery of eternity.

Contents

Foreword

Chris Duffett has asked me to write a foreword to his adventurous and imaginative creation of the life of Philip the evangelist based on the fascinating information about him in the New Testament, and I'm delighted to oblige.

Some Christians are suspicious of fiction, especially when it fleshes out a biblical account. Yet when it is constrained by historical and biblical information and filled with sound theology, as this is, I think any suspicion is unfounded. In fact such fiction has its place. For one thing it gives readers encouragement to immerse themselves in God's Word – no bad thing! For another it reminds us that these are real events that happened to real people. Above all, a good story can reach minds and hearts that bare facts, however true, may not reach. It's not for nothing that Jesus used parables to engage with people.

Philip the evangelist, known to us only from the book of Acts, is a fascinating character. We first meet him in Acts 6 as part of an administrative committee set up by the apostles to resolve a squabble to do with the management of church resources. While it's the sort of everyday crisis that anyone in church leadership will have come across in some shape or form, it's hardly the most thrilling task. Yet when in Acts 8 we meet Philip again, we find him in a very different role. First he has a spectacular ministry of healing and deliverance in Samaria, and then he is summoned by an angel to share the gospel in the amazing and thrilling encounter with an Ethiopian official. This switch from the humdrum, bureaucratic and managerial role, to being a leader at the very forefront of the extraordinary and profoundly supernatural advance of the gospel, is fascinating. It's a reminder to all Christians that while we may need to do day-to-day tasks – and do them well – we should always be prepared for God to use us in a remarkable way.

There are other things the story of Philip and the early church brings to the surface. Let me briefly suggest three challenges that emerge.

There is the challenge to know a Spirit-driven *experience*. We live at a time when the church has never produced so much in the way of words.

Bookshelves and hard disks are packed with text and information, and diaries overflow with conferences and seminars. All good and all necessary. But a quiet, disconcerting question arises: has all our professionalism and learning come at a price? Do we have that experience of God – Father, Son and Holy Spirit – that the first Christians had? Where is the extraordinary awareness of spiritual reality that runs throughout the book of Acts?

There is, too, the challenge to know a Spirit-driven *evangelism*. No one needed to tell the early Christians that they had to evangelise. Nowhere in Acts or the Epistles do we find any instructions on the necessity of preaching Jesus and guidance on how to do it. Sharing the good news was just something that the first Christians did. It overflowed out of the joy and excitement of knowing Jesus. They preached the good news simply because, after what they had personally experienced, they couldn't do anything else. Would that we were all like this!

Finally, there is the challenge to possess Spirit-driven *effectiveness*. Today the Christian church is doing a lot of good, much of it quietly overlooked. Nevertheless, these accounts in Acts should make us ask ourselves how effective we really are. The old Authorised Version has a delightful rendering of the charge against some of the first Christians that is in Acts 17:6: 'These that have turned the world upside down are come hither also.' May the same accusation be made of us!

There is always a danger in considering Christian history of what might be called holy romanticism. We make the past so wonderful that we end up wishing that we had lived in such a time. But we didn't. God has placed us in the present, not in the past, and our task is to serve our generation. Yet the past can inform both our practice and our prayers. May this imagined life of Philip inspire and encourage us in both.

J. John (Revd Canon)

www.canonjjohn.com

Acknowledgements

First off, I want to thank my family who have been wonderfully supportive and incredibly understanding as I've written this book, often hidden away in my study with post-it covered walls and hours spent in deliberation as to how and what to write. Seth, Bea and Milly you blow me away, especially when you are asked, time and time again, whether you are embarrassed by me and what I do. I like how you coolly respond a resounding "nope – why should we?!" Good on you.

Thank you to my wife Ruth, my best friend, who has given me the time to write this and who champions my longing to grow more and more, creatively. Thank you for the stone carving course that I begrudgingly did throughout the ten weeks that I also spent carving and shaping this book. The two projects seemed to go hand in hand for a while and both became more and more beautiful as time went on. The lump of stone really did inexplicably take shape into something formed and beautiful. The words of this book started to create scenes and stories that I didn't think were possible and I hope you will be chuffed with what I've created.

Thank you to the Trustees of The Light Project for letting me have three months for a writing sabbatical to plan, research and start writing this novel. Thank you for your generosity in giving me the time to do this, and also for the time for Sabbath rest.

The growing Light Project family deserve a hearty mention of thanks, especially Glyn, who has a talent for lavishly supporting me and loving me and helping me grow as an evangelist. Thank you.

Thank you also to the Lighthouse café team in Great Gransden. When I was on my writing sabbatical you had more guests than ever before. You see, it's not just down to me.

Thank you also to the Wordsmith local writing group in Great Gransden for your wisdom, great advice and support. You were the first people I stammered my simple story out to. You really did encourage me to go for it and get it down on paper, albeit with the proper historical and geographical references. You will never know how important those little post-it notes were in helping me. They were like little cheers of encouragement. Thank you.

Thank you to all those who secretly feature in this book. I can't help but write stories that are based on encounters with strangers and friends as I seek to express my faith. Thank you for the privilege of serving you and teaching you about the one who has turned my life upside down.

Lastly, I want to thank the one whom I long to become more and more like each day. Jesus, you are worthy of the tears and the wrestling I've gone through with this simple story. You've seen it's been a painful experience getting it down, especially when my writing mojo went on a long holiday. I'm pleased it came back.

I really do love you and think the world of you. I hope that this book inspires more people to dedicate their lives to you and your cause of changing this world for the better, to make it more heaven-like.

Thank you also to the crafty skill of editing that Jonathan Langley did for this book. Above all the time patiently correcting the typos, spelling mistakes and hum-dingers your kind comments to me about the story encouraged me no end. Thank you.

Thank you to Chris Hayes of Gilead Books for the ongoing encouragement and the huge generosity in donating profits of this book to the work of The Light Project. Chris, you really have taken a risk in publishing my books and for that I am so grateful. I'm praying that the risks will pay off handsomely and that our friend Jesus will pour out his blessings upon you and Lis.

Lastly, to you dear reader. Thank you for buying this book. Or, if you haven't bought it, you may have been given it – in which case: thank you for not sticking it up somewhere on a shelf but actually opening up the pages and starting this journey. I must be very honest with you, I pray that in reading this modest story that somehow you may encounter what I have as a Christian. I believe it is so good.

Introduction

Bill was drinking Rosé wine in the Wetherspoon's pub. Alone. Perched on one of those high bar-stools with elbows rested on the high table. Chin in hand. It wasn't the fact that it was just after ten in the morning that made it unusual, it was that most blokes in the pub at that time of the day drink real ale. He looked somewhat strange and out of place with his large glass of pink wine glowing proudly in the middle of the table.

I went around the tables as usual, placing our prayer beer mats on them, a job I did most Fridays, and when I eventually got to Bill's table, I asked him what he was up to. He explained how he was waiting to get a bus and see his son and grandchild for the weekend. He looked nervous and it turned out he hadn't seen them for a little bit. As he lifted the glass to his lips I noticed that his hand had a black brace on it, the kind with velcro straps and metal bits. I asked him about it and he told me how, six months previously, he had dropped a heavy garden ornament on his fingers and they had been crushed. He said he was in a great deal of pain with them.

I found myself explaining to him that I prayed for people to be healed in the name of Jesus and asked whether he wanted me to pray for his hand. He agreed and held his hand up towards me. I was somewhat surprised by his eagerness and asked if he wanted me to pray there and then. He said that he was happy for me to.

While I was praying he said that a warm sensation had gone through his hand and with that he started moving his fingers. He explained that he hadn't been able to bring his thumb up to touch his fingers before being prayed for, and now he had all the flexibility back!

He kept moving and wriggling his fingers and appeared to be in some kind of shock. I explained to him that it was a sign that God knew him and loved him.

A few minutes later I introduced him to Dave, who is one of my amazing chaplaincy team who hang out with me most Fridays in the pub to show and tell good news. The man explained to Dave what had happened and that he was now able to move his hand, and was freely showing him his new hand movements!

I offered him a book, a copy of Luke's gospel which he was happy to receive and enthused about how he would read it.

We shared the story with one of the regulars that we see week-in, week-out. This in turn led us to pray for his leg and to lay hands on him. In the pub. He explained that he felt a great warmth as I prayed and even though his leg wasn't healed he was very happy to be prayed for.

Later on in the day, as Dave and I tucked into some curry for lunch, we prayed for some words from God's heart for the man whose leg we had prayed for. I had a picture of him on a green bicycle and having so much fun. I shared this with him and he spoke about how much he used to love his little green bike as a boy and he remembered it so well. This picture led to us sharing some prophetic words with him, and even though he had drunk a few pints by this time he seemed to soak it all in. And love it.

Two weeks later, Bill came back to say thank you with his new and improved hand. He had travelled some distance to come back so that he could express his thanks to us. He also wanted to know more about

Jesus. He explained that the hospital had dismissed him from their care and were "perplexed." His wife thought it wonderful and was amazed at how her husband's hand had been made 100% completely better – and was very happy that he could now help around the house!

It's such an adventure doing what I do. I'm so grateful that I get to share and show the best news this world has ever been graced with. One of the ways that I can keep doing what I do is because of the inspiration I receive from the story of Philip.

For me, the little he is mentioned is by far the best-preached part of the Bible. I have taken his story and used it time and time again to teach others. It really is a 'life text' for me. Let me try and explain why Philip is my Bible hero.

Firstly: like him, I'm an evangelist. I've been one for most of my life – over 20 years – and I still passionately believe in my role as one, despite its awkwardness and clumsiness in trying to explain to people what it means. I always seem to have to bring disclaimers to people who think they know what it entails. Somehow they imagine that I stand on street corners holding an oversized black leather Bible, yelling at people. Yet, with all its misunderstandings and incorrect perceptions, I still believe in what I do and in the title of 'evangelist.'

Secondly, Philip reminds me that I am not alone. I work full time for The Light Project as well as being an ordained evangelist within the Baptist Union of Great Britain. I must be honest, at times it can feel a bit lonely being an evangelist. And while I know more people who are now recognising their primary call for ministry is to those who have yet to hear the gospel or be part of 'church' I need reminding time and time again that what I do and who I am is something that is good to do and I am not alone!

Philip helps me to get to that place. You see, he is the only person in the entire Bible to be called 'an evangelist'. Ever. The reference is made when Paul, quite late on in his life, goes and stays with him. Luke, the writer of the story, in his account of the Early Church recounts this in one very teeny tiny verse: "Leaving the next day, we reached Caesarea and stayed at the house of Philip the evangelist, one of the Seven." Acts 21:8

That simple verse is only the third time we encounter Philip in the Bible. The most famous scripture is when he meets an Ethiopian Eunuch. The first time is in Acts 6, when Philip is appointed as a Deacon to help the distribution of the bread after the church in Jerusalem is joined by many Greek speaking Jews from the Jewish diaspora.

So, this book is based upon three small stories of the Bible that give us a glimpse into the life of Philip. In all, this book is shaped around twenty-four verses of the Bible. Twenty-four. That's it. Let me put that in perspective: In the New Testament there are seven thousand, nine hundred and fifty seven verses! I've written this book based around a handful of them. The rest is made up. Although I have researched the geography, dates, customs and stories of the time of Philip, all the bits in between Philip being a deacon, him meeting a Eunuch and Paul visiting him later on in life... well, they're all my imagination and creativity.

With that in mind please don't get upset with me. This book is not meant to mirror the New Testament. This book isn't meant to be a biblically accurate theological treatise or historical document. It is, at the end of the day, a novel. So please enjoy it as such. I'm confident you will.

As well as all profits from the book sales going towards the work of The Light Project, there is an opportunity to partner with us and regularly support our work by becoming a friend of The Light Project.

You can find a form at the back of this book for you to fill in and send to us or follow the online link. Please do consider supporting us – any gifts you send will go directly to letting more and more people know about Jesus.

Our goal is to reveal Jesus and multiply more evangelists. Your support will help us train up and release more Philip-like characters, men and women who will go to places and dare to share the best news this world has ever been graced with.

Philip

A Novel

1

The Wave

AD 79, 66 years old

When I was a young boy, I would swim down and touch the bottom of the river. My fingertips would brush the dark, murky sediment. I was the only one who could do this, and while I pretended it didn't hurt, the pain in my ears was intense. I would feel the pressure then, but this was nothing like that. Nothing. It was anguish. Like the sides of my head where physically breaking.

I covered them as tightly as I could with the flats of my palms. The scream once more dulled by them for no-one to hear. I was the only one to feel my scream under the cold dirty sea water. It vibrated in my chest and burned in my throat. All around me, dark shapes of boats and broken trees passed by and, as I was shunted by an old fishing boat, I was drawn down deeper and deeper into the roar and rage of the wave. Opening my eyes hurt but I had to keep them wide open. I needed to get up out from the depths. But couldn't. My legs were tired. So tired. There was no other way to get air but to swim, but my legs wouldn't co-operate. There was no strength to swim up for salvation.

The wave had come quickly. All I could do was stand with open arms and wait for it to embrace me as others sprinted past to higher heights. I remained rooted, fixed to the spot like a statue. It felt like this was meant to be. And even though my toes curled and dug into the soft sand – a pathetic anchor trying to take root just before the wave engulfed me – I knew I was in the right place at the right time. I knew that this was my time to die. It felt strangely familiar and right, like I had been there before and knew of its coming. Fighting it was futile. The deep peace inside me remained very present, like a solid gold shield within me. Despite the pain.

For a moment, the wave held me on the beach and crushed me like the weight of a hundred hands, pressing all around me, pushing like a wrestler intent on the prize. I had been there to marvel. Like the others staring at the multitude of things that the retreating sea had revealed. A scattering of all kinds of debris. Old, forgotten boats. Lost nets, rust-worn anchors and even circular mill stones. It was as I gazed and watched the town's children glean amongst the gnarled wood that the towering wave appeared, unannounced. Quickly and silently. Well, without sound at first. And then it made its presence known with an intense, mighty roar. The beach around me became dark as the size of the towering wave blocked the sun and, as I looked around me, the entire town became strangely overcast in a purple-grey shadow.

I stood on the beach and the wave towered above. It stayed frozen as if stuck and watching Caesarea for what seemed like an age, contemplating its destruction and sizing up its prize. The wave behaved like it had time to gawp and consider carefully that which it would engulf first. It felt as if it was me that it was looking at. And as I looked up the full height of the grey and brown frost-topped mountain, I knew that it would become my grave.

When it crashed upon me, smothering me, I could hear a clicking sound that reverberated around my head as the water pressure made my neck pop and snap and the sheer volume of the wave slammed me first to the sand of the beach and then picked me up and threw me against the old harbour wall.

Our four girls had warned us about this day. Not just us, but everybody they met. Even as very little children, the four of them (with the twins taking the lead and the other two following) would prophesy that the flood and the big wave were coming and that people needed to get right with God. After a few years the townsfolk grew tired of their urgent warnings. Each of the four spoke with such intensity and conviction that many families moved away. It started before any of them were six years old. They would suddenly announce in the market square the coming doom of the town. It was when they started pointing at individuals and predicting their demise that it got too much even for us and we had to teach them how to use their precious gift of prophecy wisely.

That was nearly twenty years ago, and I could still picture and hear our daughters in my mind's eye the very first time they spoke about it – getting up long before dawn to wake us with the desperate words, "Mummy, Daddy, a flood is coming! Jesus says the town will be covered by a wave!" All four had heard Jesus speak about it.

As I hung there, pressed against the lower slippery wall of the harbour, I thanked Jesus that now the girls had all grown up and moved away, called to announce good news, just like we had done all our lives. They had followed in our footsteps and become adventurers for the good news. While they were planting churches in distant lands, I had lived alone in Caesarea after my wife had died. Never lonely, I always had something to do in teaching the many visitors who came to stay and learn from the years that I had served Jesus across Samaria and Israel.

He swam in front of me. Beautifully strong and like the day I saw him in the market square when he told me to go down to the desert road. It was him. He hadn't changed. Unmistakably him. After all these years of longing to meet him again, he was here. His eyes were gold and brown and his kind face with the golden flecks sparkled through the brown cloudy water, and although we were both submerged, the water didn't affect him. He looked dry.

"Take my hand, Philip," he commanded, his words echoing around me as if I were in a wine cellar. I reached out, wondering how I was hearing his voice so strongly and clearly in the pulsing swell. "Everything is going to be alright," he smiled. He swam strongly, but instead of going up, he led me deeper into the flood.

He turned to me. "It's alright, brother, everything really is going to be all right."

Brother! Why was an angel calling me brother, I thought.

And as if he had heard me he answered, "I've been sent to fetch for you. I'm taking you home."

He turned and smiled. As we swam deeper, I saw scenes from my years on earth, painted in still-life.

Like an exhibition, large colourful paintings to the left and right. Scenes with rich hues and glorious sounds. I saw the river. I wanted to linger and see my old friends again, people whose lives had been transformed. To reach out to my girls, my mum, to experience once more their laughter. I longed to stop and talk, and to see Sarah again. But I knew it was my time to go home and she would be waiting for me. It was time to enter into that very kingdom that I had pleaded with others to prepare for.

The scenes looked good and as I watched I thanked God for all that he had done in my life.

My name is Philip, and this is my story.

2

The River

AD 26, 12 years old

The bright green, dancing plants stubbornly bedded themselves in the steady flow, they never stopped moving and we were entranced by them. Often our gaze sank deep in the clear river watching the small fish dart in-between. The plants dance never repeated; they had familiar moves but in a myriad of ways. When the sun shone through them they looked translucent, yet they were never torn by the course of the river. So delicate, yet so strong.

Apart from during the Sabbath, we played most days by the deep river lined with the swaying brown reeds. It was solace. Quiet. It was ours.

In silence, we would look, soak it in and simply wait. And that was all right. No pressure to do, say, or perform. We could just be and enjoy the babble of the moving water and allow its melody to sweep over us. To soothe us. It was in these times that I felt the strongest and I forgot the things that made me sigh, the heaviness that burdened me as I got up in the morning. The deep weight that I carried, that caused my neck to bow and ache daily, was cast out at these moments. Those deep sighs were banished in this place and it was only when returning home that they, too, somehow returned home with me. It was as if the deep sigh that I was delivered of when I ventured to our river caught up with me once more and clung to my chest when I stepped back into my home. I wished I could bury it forever in the river.

Times at the river were snippets of purified peace, of being replenished. When I had to skip them for whatever reason, I would become irritable, as if I had to carry an even more awkward weight upon my back. But for now I allowed the river to lullaby me and I lingered as long as I could, waiting for her cheery voice, the one that would snap me out from my daydream with a shrill challenge to swim or play. Then we would both spring up and jump in and pretend to be like the darting fish, me a perch and she a pike, swim-chasing in-between the dainty, hair-like, green swaying plants. She would grab my feet and I would scream and splutter in the water as she would bite my toes pretending to eat her victim.

As long as we didn't place our feet accidentally in the silty river bottom it remained crystal clear. One slip and a bubble of brown, dank sediment would engulf us. If the word 'old' had a smell, it would smell like those slight slips off a rock. One mistimed swim to where you thought a rock would be and a cloud of old would cover you. Years of silt, of well-travelled rotted leaves, would hide our naked brown bodies.

I found freedom in the water. On land, my right foot refused to cooperate with the rest of me and I half shuffled, half limped out of the water. But in it I was unrestricted. Ever since I was seven years old, 'Lame-dog' was the name that I was most often called. It would ring in my ears as the other children pointed and mocked me. This happened most days – unless I hid inside, which is hard to do when there are many errands. If I did try to hurry to get the jobs done, the others would point and jeer even more, as I would jerk the right side of my body to get anywhere more quickly. And it wasn't just the children who would mock and point.

She never laughed at me. She had a beautiful knack of not even noticing and I don't ever recall a time when she had even looked at my foot or asked me about it. Besides, she was the only one who had seen me swim – and compared to the way I walked, I swam like a fish! When I stumbled and fell, she would just gently place her hands under my arm pits and around my shoulders and hoist me up as if doing so was the most natural thing in the world, as if all friends did that sort of lifting all the time! Her strength made me feel strong. Sometimes I would fall on purpose just so that I could feel her strength close to me.

The care wasn't all one way. I never teased her about the Samaritan heritage that the other children spat at her about. What did it matter to me if she was a Samaritan? Of course, I was familiar with the stories of the hundreds of years of fighting, the tales of bloodshed that all Jewish boys spoke about. I knew about the murders and was told to stay away from 'those scum.' But she wasn't like those described in the ugly stories. She was kind. Besides, she was my Sarah. My best friend.

On this day I had to be quick. I didn't tell her at first, as I knew she would be disappointed, but it needed to be a nippy dip or Mum would ask way too many questions. She needed help. Again. Like she always did, but today especially, so that she was way worse than usual and hadn't managed to get up in the morning. I had never known my mum to be 'well.' On most days she was able to get up at least for a bit. But not today. Mum had been unwell since my birth.

That's when she had nearly died. Like my pathetic ankle, I had never known any difference when it came to my mum. They weren't able to have any more children after me, but rather than being spoilt and having everything done for me as the only child, I was the one to carry, fetch and make money when I could. I had to grow up quickly.

Dad was away for long stretches at a time working on the trading boats in and out of Dor. On the rare times he was home he would sit me on his knee and regale me with tales of sailing to Italy trading leather or dried fruits and spices. The boats were small, manned by just a few. We all knew of the dangers and, while our fears remained unspoken in our home, I carried the uncertainty of whether I would see him again when he ventured off to work. Each time, I took a deep breath and made a wish that he would come home safely. He always did.

I had a routine for every day he was gone when I walked out from our home. I would pause by the gate facing east towards the coast, and it was at these times, leaning on the old wooden gate, that my heart longed for safety and for my dad to come home. I would breathe a kind of prayer asking for the waves to be kind and that the sea wouldn't become his grave.

Don't get me wrong, while I longed for him to be home I didn't find it hard being the man about the house in his absence. I always took the opportunities that came my way, especially at festival times when I would venture up to the great city and help sell the doves and manage the queues for the money changers. Mum and Dad called me 'the most winsome boy in the world' as I always managed to get money together when we needed it. Never out of pity or by begging, but always through working hard and finding the most lucrative jobs around for a young lad to do.

It was while I was contemplating how I would tell Sarah that today's swim would be a short one that she took off her outer garment, the one with the embroidered red and green flower on it and quickly, like usual, whipped her loin cloth over her head. I looked at her body and she caught me staring. Making herself small by pulling her elbows low and placing her hands together as a mini- shield she snapped:

"Oi! What you looking at?" I blinked. Then shook my head slightly.

"Looking at? Nothing..." I stumbled, and then quickly blurted, "I mean: nothing except a loser who can't beat me to Herod's Rock!"

And with that I tore off my well-worn brown loin cloth dived into the cool, sweet water and swam as fast as I could to the rock that stood proud in the middle of the river. I didn't need to turn to check if she was following. I knew she would be hot on my tail. She was the stronger swimmer. By far. I had yet to beat her to the rock this year. It used to be easy when we were younger, but she had grown quicker and stronger than me. A last few frantic strokes and I would be there. Through the bubbling sound of the water I heard her taunt.

"You swim like a bathing sparrow!" she jeered, standing astride the rock waving her arms crazily like wings and jerking her head like a bird. I was well and truly beaten. Again. With her sparrow impression finished, I caught another glimpse. She looked different, and her new shape intrigued me. So that I wouldn't get caught looking again, I flipped onto my back and stared up at the clouds drifting in the midday turquoise blue as I also drifted slowly in the river's current. I shouted: "Well, I always let little girls win!" With that she jumped high and the strength of the water-bomb knocked me off my back.

"Sarah! You nearly landed on me! That's so dangerous!" I choked and complained at the same time and she laughed as she swam back to the edge of our river and clambered onto the smooth, dark rocks.

Drying off on them didn't take long. They soaked up the sun and retained their warmth late into the night. Once, we stayed out all night with the warm smooth boulders as our beds. Recently I had left a mid-swim snack of four figs on them and when we returned from playing they were all gooey and partly cooked.

"I have to go in a bit and help my mum" I eventually had the courage to say. Her brown big eyes looked sad.

"Ohhh, Philip, why?" she whined. "What about some fishing?"

"My mum's not doing too well today. She needs help fetching some firewood and our neighbour has asked if I would help grind some of the corn too, and.... and..." I trailed off with my explanation. Of course there were also another dozen jobs that needed doing, but I left the explanation hanging. Nothing else was said as we dried on the rock until she gently asked:

"Are you worried about her?"

The sadness in her eyes from losing her play pal so early on in the day had changed to kindness.

No-one had ever asked me how I actually felt about my mum. No-one. Her question caused a warm painful ache in my chest. It felt unfamiliar and, as I tried working out what the pain was, my eyes filled with tears.

"Sorry," I said simply, and with that I closed them, wishing I could vanish from Sarah's concern. Closing my eyes didn't help. It caused big tears to roll down my cheeks. I opened my eyes to see her right in front of me, her long damp dark hair framing her caring, beautiful face. "Philip, I'm so sorry. Everything will be alright, you know. Come on."

And with that reassurance she leant forward and kissed me on my lips and reached to put her hands under my arm pits, like she did when I fell. She placed her string hands around my shoulders and gently pulled me up and held me for a few seconds. My back straightened as I stood held by her. Unable to reciprocate. Unsure of what to do and how, I wanted to return the embrace but my arms wouldn't behave and do what I wanted them to do. Breaking the awkwardness, she gently whispered: "Go, on, soft lad... you had better go. We don't want your mummy to worry about you now, do we?"

"See you tomorrow," I mumbled as I hobbled off, and as I walked I also dressed myself. She stood on our rock.

"Yep, same time, same place. Bring some treats!" she called after me.

I carried on walking as strongly as I could, but my limp caused my temporarily paralysed arms to sway as I walked away. Coupled with trying to get my arms into the sleeves of my inner garment I must have looked a right sight, and with embarrassment I managed to awkwardly wave one hand in the air in agreement without looking back.

Out of eyesight and just in time, the emotions flooded out. I leant upon a tree trunk and buried my face in the rough bark and wept and returned the embrace I so much wished I had been able to give a few minutes before. As I hugged that tree I thought of her kind words.

And that kiss.

My first kiss.

Mum hadn't got up. She was still sleeping and looked paler than usual. I placed the wood I had gathered by the door and poured her some water in an earthen goblet that dad had taught me to make. I had gotten used to intricate jobs like this. I had dug out the clay by the river, but, as we didn't have a kiln, we had to exchange some bread with our neighbours, who allowed us occasional use of theirs – if they had room when firing goblets or bowls. I had become pretty good at pottery. Well, good enough to keep us stocked with three of everything we needed.

We never had visitors, so three of everything was always enough. Just as well that the ancient Jewish law wouldn't allow guests, otherwise I would have more pottery jobs to do! Mum had never stopped bleeding from the time when I was born, sometimes heavy but mostly just a steady slow flow. I knew that the blood flow differed as I was the one who had to clean the rags. The bloody water would have different shades depending on how unwell she had been. This week was bad. Really bad. Dark, dark red-brown water. On weeks like this she often fainted.

Much of dad's earnings had been spent on doctors, their time as well as their different remedies, yet the flow of blood had never completely stopped. Once, he even arranged for a travelling physician from Egypt to be brought to the house. I squinted my eyes thinking of him and the layers of bright clothes he wore. He had layers upon layers of the most vibrant cloth, woven gold, making patterns of eagle heads and moons and stars. We could have bought an Ox with the price of the medicine and consultation: 150 dinars! It didn't make a mite of difference, though. And, if anything, the disappointment seemed to make mum worse. Bloody doctors! Even the Pharisees' prayers of healing hadn't worked and we were told, after we had paid them a 'gift' for their time and trouble, that it was our sin that was to blame. Apparently they declared that it was something sinful mum had done, or possibly her parents, which had caused the sickness. Their vagueness of who was to blame just brought more shame upon our family.

As I looked at my mum sleeping on the simple wooden bed, I bowed my head and felt that weight return again upon my back and neck. They all had no idea how hard I and my dad had to work and how getting money to pay for them had been the catalyst for dad having to accept work away for weeks or months at a time. Dangerous work, at that.

"Those dogs" I said under my breath, covering my mouth to muffle my anger. Mum stirred but then continued to sleep. The flowers I had placed next to her bed yesterday bowed over towards her as if in a watchful gaze. She was a good mum. Even though it pained her, there were times we could walk together, not far and never hand in hand. But at least we walked together and mum would reach over and gently ruffle my black, wiry, thick hair and say: "What a handsome young man you are!" I had my dad's short bulky build, but I had her eyes. Bluey grey eyes, which caught the light and looked like glimpses of the sky, just before it rained, she said. Which was rare where we lived. Rare like the colour of our eyes.

By association, I had worked out from an early age that I also was made impure by her illness. The other mums ushered their children away or would draw their cloaks around them like hens gathering chicks when they saw me approach. The mums never said anything unkind to me, it just kind of happened instinctively. Every one naturally kept away from that which would make them unclean, and I was unclean because of my mum. However, not all the children would keep away from me and, beyond the watchful eyes of their mums, some would risk shoving me or poking me with sticks, even though they were told to keep well away, it was most weeks that the taunting also came with a beating of some kind.

The poking sticks and punches I could just about handle. It was that name that cut me. Each jeer made me angry and, depending on how mum was, sometimes I would lash out uncontrollably at the jeer of 'Lame-dog'. Mostly if she was particularly ill and I was particularly worried about her. It was these moments – of punching faces and jeering children, breaking noses and scratching at eyes – that got me in the biggest trouble when my dad came home. He never beat me, but he would take away treats. And when you don't have many, that hurts. The harshest punishment was not being allowed out to play. That meant not going to the river. Which meant no swimming with my Sarah.

Mum stirred again but didn't notice me standing by the door and, after turning on to her side, the slower breaths of sleep started again.

As I watched her I began day dreaming again. I always felt I was to blame. I had never dared tell mum or dad or ask them whether I was or not. This conversation was a private one, just in my head, which happened most nights. I would gaze up to the stars as I laid upon my wooden pallet bed and think about that big question: what if I had never been born? Mum would have never been sick. I felt like I was a mistake and my birth had caused misery upon misery to my parents. And to me. Lame-dog.

There were more jobs to be done and I knew my neighbours were wanting me to help turn the heavy wheel to grind more corn. Alone.

And that was the ache I carried. Alone. Because of my mum's illness I was rarely held by her. The invisible, unclean barrier kept us at arm's length. When I fell as a child and grazed my knee I would jump into her arms but, now that I had had my Bar mitzvah and was a man, I had long forgotten what it was to be held.

Until Sarah's embrace. The sensation I felt by the river came back and tears started to flow again as I recalled that moment of kindness. Being held. I shook my head and wiped away the tears and glanced at mum and I dared to say, softly, "thank you God. You have given me hope today. I dare to believe that everything will be all right." Just as Sarah had said.

3

The Honey

I was late and she was waiting. To make matters worse, I hadn't brought any treats.

"Oh, it's you. I was getting scared," she said and as I walked closer she continued, "I thought I heard someone from the trees and it felt creepy."

She nodded her head towards the small wooded area behind me. My arrival made her smile and her shoulders visibly dropped down in relief as she looked at me. Her fear must have been genuine, most unlike my Sarah to be afraid. Of anything.

"Frightened of a little cuddly wuddly bear in a little boo-boo tree, are we?" My baby teasing impression made her laugh, and being late didn't seem to matter anymore. The lack of snacks went unnoticed. We took our time and swam, mixed in the usual games with an adapted version of hide and seek, which I won royally with the help of an old hollow reed that I breathed through while clinging to a submerged rock with my knees, poking it above the surface of the river, undetected for over five minutes.

When Sarah eventually did find me, her frightened expression had returned. She explained that awful feeling of someone watching. Yet she wasn't certain that she had seen anyone. Wishing to take her mind off the worry I chirped: "Come on let's find some treats!"

I had overheard the neighbour's children boasting about finding a hive in the old sycamore tree by the dried up well, only ten minutes' walk from our river. I knew exactly where it was and their bragging would be to my benefit! Sarah loved the idea of exploring, especially as we both had a sweet tooth and the thought of sucking on honeycomb was enough to make our eyes turn big and round and we both made funny mmmmmm noises at each other in anticipation.

The nest was exactly where the neighbour's children had bragged about it. Beneath it was evidence that others, too, had tried to harvest the sweet treasure within the old Sycamore. At its base were rocks, sticks and a curious-looking net on a branch. It had been a handsome tree in its prime, but now it stood with a stoop, half the limbs dried and dead, and it was in one of the hollowed out dried up branches that the bees had made their home. The low buzzing sound confirmed this, as did the regular to-ing and fro-ing of the worker bees. They seemed content enough and for a while we watched them and gave nick-names to a few. After surveying the tree by pacing around and around, and with neck-ache from the deliberations while looking up, we decided that the best course of action was to break open the branch from below and steal the honey comb from the base, rather than trying the other children's tactic of using force at the entrance. The scattering of crude implements revealed that children must have downed tools and run away in a hurry, perhaps stung by the protective swarm. We needed to be careful.

The branch was too high to reach, and not having a strong ankle proved to be the deciding factor in who should sit upon whose shoulders to prise open the base of the branch. Sarah lifted me high and bowed her head to enable me to sit firmly upon her shoulders.

"My God, boy! You're a chunky monkey!" she exclaimed, making a funny raspberry sound while taking my weight.

I didn't mind her banter in the slightest and retorted, "Sarah, he's not just your God, you know, and besides it's not me who's heavy, it's just you are such a weed."

And with that, Sarah staggered about pretending to not take my weight, all the time giggling. She manoeuvred me beneath the nest and slowly bent down to reach a sharp edged rock as I held the top of her head.

"Use this to wedge the nest open," she whispered.

"Really? You don't want me to negotiate and offer this bit of flint in exchange for half a jar of honey?" I said loudly. Even in the messing around, the bees were uninterested and carried on in their routine, buzzing in and out. We remained unnoticed by them, and that was just fine by us.

Hammering the base would startle the bees and we would surely get stung, so instead I gently wedged the flint below, in between bits of bark, and with both hands I started to move the dried branch apart. For a dead branch it was stubbornly strong. The flint sat heavily in the palm of my hand as I considered how the next gentle move needed to lever open the obstinate wood to reveal the treasure within. Its weight and feel brought to mind a primeval thought of using it as hard as I could. As a hammer on the branch. Surely just once wouldn't hurt, I reasoned.

The effect was immediate and with the thwack of flint on wood still ringing in my ears Sarah screamed: "Beeeeeeeeeees!"

The shriek was accompanied by sharp pain over and over in my right armpit. I quickly threw the stone away to enable me to brush away the bees causing the sting and, as I did, I tumbled off Sarah's shoulders and landed hard on the ground. "Run!" I cried. Sarah picked me up in her usual strong way and lifted me onto my feet. The bees were all around us and sharp pains came again and again onto my neck, ears and arms. Being stung once was bad enough, but over and over was unbearable.

It was only when we got fifty metres or so away that the bees, seemingly tired from the chase and the stinging, stopped. But it was too late. We were both hurt and as we brushed off the dying bees who had deposited their stings in us we both looked apologetically at each other.

"Shall we try again with the hammering?!" Sarah chirped as I sucked air in-between my teeth and with each breath tried to hold back the tears. It was painful and my response to her sarcasm wasn't kind.

"Well it was your idea, woman!" and with that we looked at each other and burst into laughter. "Woman?!" Sarah snorted as she laughed with me. "Why thank you, man!" She laughed. "Now come on, Philip, let's go and cool these stings off." She reached for my hand and led me on the path back to our river. The pain receded with that simple touch. I had missed holding my mum's hand and walking with Sarah in this way brought reassurance and peace to me that I had simply forgotten how it could feel. I didn't feel alone. Yes, stung and in pain, but not alone.

Longing to jump into the cool waters, we stood at the side and stared at the strange package on our rock. We resisted tearing off our clothes to bathe the stings but rather stood gazing at the brown leather pouch, loosely tied. It sat right upon our rock. Right in the middle.

"I told you someone was here," Sarah exclaimed holding my hand tightly. I scanned around, darting my eyes left and then right, and turned to pan behind us.

"Listen, whoever was here must have forgotten their small bag of whatever, and I can ask around and see who it belongs to."

The 'whatever' was honeycomb. A crudely written note was written in charcoal upon the rock: 'a gift for you two' it said. Sarah stood shaking her head sternly looking at the gift and at me.

"Put it down please, Philip. You don't know who left it and we shouldn't touch it." I placed the bag down in the position we had discovered, nudged it to its original spot and placed my hands on my hips waiting for Sarah to tell me what I should do. Some of the honey had dribbled onto my fingers and I instinctively lifted them to my lips and licked them. It tasted good. Really good.

"It obviously isn't poisonous – look I've tried some."

Sarah was still shaking her head as she exclaimed, "I mean, who leaves gifts of honey on rocks?"

For over a year now the river had been ours. Our safe haven. We had met by accident back then, we both just so happened to be searching for solace and both ended up sitting at either side of the rock that the honey now crowned, without realising the other was there. That was until she threw a stone into the river. And that's how we had met. By accident. Searching for head space, we had each found a friend.

"How about we enjoy the honey and bury the bag and deny any knowledge of it if anyone asks?!" I said confidently. Sarah agreed and soon her fear of the strange gift was calmed as we ravished the honey comb and giggled about our bee hive adventure. After counting up the stings it turned out I had far more than her. "It's because I'm sweeter," I teased.

After a cooling swim it was time to go home and we scrambled off our rock that had held our surprise gift. The sweet honey had made our cheeks glow red. It had been such a treat and we giggled and scampered up the path towards the village home. Mum would be wondering where I had been. Explaining the red bumps that adorned my neck and arms was going to be tricky. If she noticed.

He stood on the path, towering high. He was well over six feet. The sun silhouetted his chiselled, shaven face and for a moment all we could see was a black shape on what was obviously a large soldier's body. He wasn't armed. He looked strangely out of place alone. There was no sign of other soldiers on patrol, yet he wore the colour of the Herodian king Antipas. He looked intently at us and we froze. As I observed him, my head tilted to the left. The man looked oddly wonky. Where the right ear should have been was just a small hole surrounded by tiny hairy lumps.

"Get ready to run…" Sarah said under her breath. Not fancying my chances, I looked at the soldier and cleared my throat ready to say something and, as I opened my mouth ready to greet him, he asked in a low bass drum voice, "So, you got my gift then?"

Sarah grabbed my hand hard and strode around him with her head bowed and with me shuffling in tow, shouted confidently: "Yes, thank you very much, very kind of you. We must go. Bye!"

"The pleasure is all mine," he boomed. "The pleasure is all mine."

Not before we couldn't hear his raucous laughter bellowing over the gentle bubble of the river did we stop. She didn't say a word. She didn't need to. 'I told you so' was written all over her face as she stared angrily at me. It would have been frightening, but the lumps from the stings made her look strangely comical!

We agreed not to go to the river for a week. I missed it. But meeting a Roman soldier so far from his fort all by himself by our river had shaken us. We had seen soldiers before, training in the summer months, swimming by the barracks where we weren't permitted. It was off-limits to us, which was a pity, as the best fishing was to found in the deeper waters there. But a soldier by our river? Never.

It wasn't so much that he was part of the occupation of our land that bothered me, rather that this soldier was at *our* river. Our secret place. The knowledge that someone else knew of it made my heart sink. My fishing pole and simple net were stashed away by its banks. He could steal them. But, then, that was replaceable It was the feeling of being encroached upon that caused an ache in the pit of my stomach. The river was the only thing I could have really called mine. My river. Our river. I knew every rock in that stretch. They even had silly nicknames.

With the taste of the honey still in my mouth, I considered our encounter with him. It really did give a new meaning to the expression 'bitter-sweet'. Yes, the honey had tasted so good, but the happenstance meeting with the one-eared man had left me concerned. As I sat alone in the yard, I wondered whether we would ever swim to Herod's rock again. But more than that, would I get to spend time with Sarah? I hoped so. Dearly hoped so. Spending any time together in public was a no-no, and not having a secure meeting place made me feel sad. But there was no choice, it wasn't as if I could invite Sarah round to mine for a meal or to meet my mum. The shame on my family was enough without talk of a Jewish boy having a Samaritan friend.

The week passed slowly. To make matters worse, mum continued to be unwell and I spent long stretches of the day without anyone to talk to.

It felt like the longest week of my life. Seeing my Sarah again, playing, swimming and fishing, I had soon forgotten about the uninvited guest at our river.

Besides, there was no sign of him and we even checked the path for footprints and any signs of a disturbance. Moreover, the soldiers often moved from place to place, month by month, Capernaum maybe, and then shipped off to join the army in Rome via Caesarea the next.

The one-eared soldier we had met would have been part of a cohort belonging to Antipas, the son of the Great Herod, who was allowed power from the Romans. Every Jew in my village called him the great 'puppet king' and we loathed him. His soldiers would sometimes steal food from us or press-gang some of the men into carrying heavy loads for them. Antipas' soldiers were similar to those of the Roman army, and the one we had seen looked fairly old. I reassured Sarah that he must have been ready for retirement after his twenty five years of service. He would most likely have received his pension and a gift of land to farm and was well gone, never to return to our river.

A month passed. Sarah and I, as we had always done before, arranged to swim the day after the Sabbath, after I had done all my chores, which I hoped would all be done and dusted by the sixth hour, when most people hid away from the heat of the day. This was the most perfect time for a swim. But on this day the chores took longer than usual, as we were running low on provisions and more had to be done. Mum was up and feeling much better and able to cook and look after the house, but the store room was bare.

Dad wasn't due back for another few weeks and, as usual, this meant drastic measures to make a little money. While I cherished the sense of responsibility of doing jobs and earning money, I dreaded this one job.

It was a job no boy in our village would do, so on the plus side there was always plenty of it around and the money was really good, considering the effort in collecting and carrying. I prepared the old discarded leathery wine skin by sewing up an old tear and found the two pieces of old tile for the picking. The smell remained on the tiles from the previous job and I heaved. It was a mystery to me that something that stank so badly could be of vital importance in the process of curing the leather.

Collecting dog faeces rated right up there with the world's most humiliating jobs. Not as bad as the tanners themselves, who would have had to live a life of being constantly unclean having to touch dead animals six days a week. They were perpetually ritually unclean. And the stink. They said that the nose just stopped smelling and that they couldn't notice it anymore. But for the rest of us, it was putrid. Tying on my sandals I saw mum.

She had been watching me get the implements ready and smiled as she said gently, "Without leather, you wouldn't have those sandals, Philip."

I loved it when Mum had a gentle and wise word to share with me. Often my coming and going from the home would be unnoticed, so I was happy for her to say anything to me.

I responded: "Yes, I know. It's just the smell I can't get used to, and I'm sure Peter the carpenter's dog has been eating rats again. Trying to collect his dung is a bit tricky when all I want to do is puke!"

3. The Honey

I play acted the scene of bending over with the dirty tiles and retching as I did. Mum smiled, but didn't quite make a laugh. She was still weak and the morning's brushing and tidying had taken their toll.

"Thank you for what you do Philip, I'm really proud of you, son."

And with that, she stepped back into the shadows of her room to lay down. Again. I closed my eyes and imagined a hug from her. This made me think of Sarah once more. While she hadn't hugged me since the time I cried, it still felt close and recent. Thinking of her helped me hurry to collect the dog dung so that I could swim with her.

Situated to the south east of the village where the prevailing winds would carry the stench of rotting hides and diluted dog dung for the curing, Judas the Tanner would literally pay me good money for crap. He was a simple man with few words and a long, dirty, dark brown beard that rested stickily half way down his chest. His baldness gave him the impression that somehow his head was upside down, but I didn't dare tease him about it. Besides, he always paid me well. Very well. I don't think it was out of pity for me he paid me so handsomely. Yet I must have looked a sorry sight with my weak ankle and the characteristic way I limped up to his gate, surrounded by flies as they swarmed at the old sack of dog mess that I had faithfully filled. I would always wash the coin he gave me afterwards. His hands were always dirty. Ingrained with grime. It looked like they had both been tattooed with a deep pattern of filth.

A couple of hours of collecting would pay the same as what some of the young men received who worked in the vineyard for a whole day. With my Dinar piece stowed away safely in my money pouch I headed to the river via dropping off the old wine skin and slates. I was late and didn't have time to wash, besides I would soon be jumping in the river and cleaning myself.

She wasn't on our rock as usual, but in the river already, standing waist-deep in the water. Even though it was the hottest part of the day, she appeared to be shivering. I quickly undressed and jumped in, causing a wave to splash over her face. But there was no playful response. She didn't splash me back. She didn't even look back at me but just stood with her arms wrapped around her chest. I chirped,

"Sorry I was late, I had to collect dog doo again."

She stood still, other than her shivering she was like a statue gazing into the water. "How come you're cold, you're shivering!" There was still no response. I stood close on the rock opposite and saw the scratches on her arms and with the river water dripping from her face I thought I also saw tears, although there was no sound coming from her.

The water around her waist was murky but it didn't look like the old brown sludge from the river bed but more like when I had to do the washing of the clothes and the old rags mum used to mop up that steady flow that made her so sick. "Sarah, you're bleeding!" I cried. I figured she must have cut herself when swimming. It was then that I saw the bluey purple bruise. Like teeth marks. On her shoulder. I reached out to touch her shoulder but she recoiled sharply.

"Sarah, what happened?" I asked. "Tell me, why are you bleeding?"

"He was here." She said coldly, and with a long pause between her words she looked at me with her beautiful brown big eyes flowing with tears and said, "we should have never eaten the honey."

4

My Revenge

There was only one soldier with one ear that had been seen around Capernaum: Marcus Aurelius. He was part of the Herodian king Antipas' battalion and had also done a spell as a temple guard in Jerusalem previous to that. Before that, no-one knew. It was the old-timers who recognised my description of him. At the temple, his sharp tongue and rough attitude had given him a reputation as a man to watch out for at the festivals. He was one that the seasoned traders had grown accustomed to avoiding. As I had worked out by his age, it was true that he was coming to the very end of his service as a soldier. No doubt he was preparing for his cosy retirement and handsome reward from Rome with a little plot of land and farm in the empire. I had other plans for him. I was going to find him. I was going to kill him.

Despite my rage, I was clever enough to realise that this needed careful preparation, and while my chest ached with a fiery desire to kill, I knew I had to hold back and plan it meticulously. A kneejerk reaction would have felt good for a fleeting moment, but I would have ended up dead. Over the afternoon I had acted out killing him in my mind a thousand times, and with each daydream I felt the pleasure of seeing him grasp for breath before my eyes, but despite my imagination running away with me I knew that he could easily break me like a twig with his bare hands.

If I hunted him down now, I would be killed. Besides, I had done very little in-between sitting by the gate of the yard and weeping silently while mum remained in her room. I had checked on her and poured some wine into one of the crude grey goblets I had made and left it beside her bed. She was fast asleep and I reached for her shoulder under the brown blanket that lay loosely upon her to check her temperature and also to gently stroke it, wishing I had been able to reach out and reassure Sarah a few hours previously.

Mum didn't wake that day and I left her to sleep. The sickness was taking its toll on her and a few hours being up and around in the morning was about her limit these days. We needed dad home but he needed to work to pay the bills that the doctors kept invoicing. We had very little left. Mum had left some bread and vegetables out for me. Usually I would be ravenous after a long day of work and play but I couldn't eat and just picked at the flat bread and then left it.

I ran the afternoon through my mind again. Other than those glaring words about the honey, Sarah hadn't said anything else to me, and while I pleaded with her to talk, she refused. Or couldn't. I longed to embrace her and share the comfort she had given me weeks previously, I wanted to let her know that everything would be alright, but any advance towards her caused panic and her shaking became uncontrolled. Eventually we left the river and walked back to the village in silence, Sarah ahead as I desperately tried to keep up.

When Sarah arrived home that afternoon, her mum had noticed straight away. The blood had soaked through and stained the middle of her dress and despite the attempts Sarah had made to clean herself in the river, the bleeding wouldn't stop. News of the attack spread around the village and while Sarah had woven a story about a couple of wild dogs that had chased and bitten her it wasn't believed. Her mum had seen this kind of thing before with some of the womenfolk in the outlying villages around Samaria, but had never imagined that it would have happened to her little girl.

I remained silent when I heard the boys next door talk about my Sarah as 'that Samaritan girl' and chat about the attack as if they were talking about the weather or the latest chariot racer in Rome. They had big mouths and I wouldn't have given a second thought to punching them in their ugly faces. But I remained silent so as to glean the news.

It turned out that one of their own Samaritan doctors had been called to examine her and an attempt was made to mend her torn body. I knew Sarah would have put up a good fight. She was strong. The very thought of it made me heave, and in the quiet of the yard as I sat alone in the cool evening, I wished I had someone to talk to about it. I had no-one. I pounded the hard-pressed worn earth around me and I wished, deeply wished, that Dad was home. I could confess to him about having a Samaritan friend and tell him all about our remote river place and what had happened today. He would know what to do. He would probably help me find Marcus and show him that people like him couldn't just take their pick of whoever they wanted and snatch them like a fig off a tree to consume. Dad would ensure that he would never do anything like that again, and I would make sure of it too. The ancient words from the Torah echoed through my mind: An eye for an eye and a tooth for a tooth. This bastard had hurt my only friend, and for that he would be sorry.

In that moment, the tears stopped and I closed my eyes tight and said the most heart-felt, lucid prayer I had ever uttered: 'Lord God, bring my dad home soon to help me kill this son of a bitch. Amen.'

It would never have been down to me that we couldn't see each other again. The previous day's attack didn't make any difference in my mind to our friendship. Why would it? If anything, I was going to be a better friend and we could always find a better spot to swim and play and I would make sure that she was never alone. I wanted to be a good friend to her and stick closer than a brother. The guilt of being late hung around my neck and shoulders. It was a dull pain. If only I had been on time. I reasoned that I would make up for being late and from now on I was going to take extra care of my best friend.

I coughed from the dust that wafted up from my awkward limp-walk, and that caused me to focus on the task at hand. I had never dared approach the outlying homes before. They belonged to those that 'we', the Jews, hated. These outsider families were only tolerated as the village elders had said that the village needed meat and they, the Samaritans, made good shepherds. No-one else would be prepared to do that work in these parts. Not only did the job make you ceremonially unclean, people had been mauled by lions and wolves before, in the pitch black of night. The profession made my dog mess gathering look like a palace gardener by comparison.

Even though I fully appreciated the trouble I would be in, I didn't care. I had decided to call round at Sarah's house and risk a beating from her family, and it would be worth it to know if she was alright. I knew that meeting me by the river would never happen again. This was the only way I was going to be able to talk with her and apologise again for being late the day before.

I knocked on the old green wooden door which opened slowly to reveal an empty kitchen and store room. It was obvious they had gone, but I still called out a customary greeting which echoed around the dark room. In the corner lay her embroidered red and green flower dress.

A sharp pain stabbed my chest and I doubled over, unable to scream but with my mouth wide open. Was she dead?

"You, boy!" a man shouted from across the street, already holding a stick in hand and drumming it into his other palm menacingly. He paced towards me. As I stood straight, I longed for words to come out of my mouth but they couldn't. Rather, I was only able to mouth words as I looked at the furious man who was striding towards me. "Please... please," I eventually stammered. "Please, sir. I don't mean any harm. I am a friend of Sarah, the girl who lives here!"

He spat his words out and on his sharp exhale shouted: "Friend? Of that slag?"

I turned, leaving him laughing with his hands on his hips and the stick lying at his feet. He laughed all the time I limped away, like that bastard one-eared soldier had done. Children ventured to the doors of their homes to see what the raucous was about and added to the man's laughter with a chorus of "lame-dog, lame-dog, lame-dog!"

It was the loud-mouthed next door boys again, gossiping in their yard who revealed Sarah was alive, but rumours had spread that she had led the soldier on and that it was really her who was the one to blame. The shame on the family had driven them away back into the heartland of Samaria. Besides, I learnt that she was pledged to be engaged to her cousin, a widower with three children all younger than her, but not by much. He owned a vineyard in Sebastia. The loud boys mocked her and said horrible things like "what use is a tarnished wife?" A handsome dowry was paid for a virgin, but very little for one who had known a man.

Sarah was gone. The pain of missing her and the weight of the guilt was slightly numbed in the knowledge that at least she was alive. "I miss you, Sarah," I breathed out into the night, wishing she could hear me.

Dad didn't come home soon like I had asked God on that painful day. But he would. I could feel it. After helping mum around the house and doing what I could to get some money together for food, I would wait each day perched on the old grey stoned wall under the weathered, worn fig tree until the sun started to go down and mum would be expecting me home. If she was up from her bed, which wasn't often. Her haemorrhage made her very tired. She spent more time in bed than out. I longed to talk to her but knew my secret friendship with Sarah would make her sad and she wouldn't have the strength to listen to what had happened.

For the next seven days I waited alone on the wall after my chores, looking east towards the road that meandered down to the coast and eventually met other paths joining the bends and turns, all the way to the town of Dor which nestled on the turquoise blue coast with a fresh breeze and fresher promise of work on board one of the countless trading boats. Being lame meant a long journey like that was way beyond me. I would never see Dor or the other places Dad described, but hearing his stories was good enough for me. I had a good imagination and in a moment I could picture myself standing by the shore, waiting for Dad to drift up in his small boat after a long days sailing.

I became alive when I heard his tales. Sitting next to him, I imagined it was me who was the one on the seas, in the precarious trade boats. I could hear the flap-flap of the red sail in the wind as Dad regaled me with his latest adventures. Even the old ones were still good to hear again. And again.

Besides waiting and daydreaming I had very little else to do. The thought of going to the river made my chest ache and my throat tighten and besides, when I did think of her it was as if an old woollen blanket covered my very being and I felt sad. Beyond sad. I felt numb. I tried desperately hard not to think of her but when I slept I dreamed of her in the river. Most nights I would wake two or three times, sometimes more, crying out for her.

It was becoming hard to imagine what I did before we played down there, before I had met her, my forbidden friend who by chance had sat on the other side of the rock. I missed her so much. Every day was an adventure with her. It was Sarah who taught me to fish, not with an old baby-ish net on the end of a flimsy stick, but proper fishing, with pole and line that always hooked a feast to take home.

It was soon after Sarah had taught me the art of fishing that she caught the ugliest looking one we had ever seen. It had whisker tentacles and a squashed looking head. I had to explain to Sarah that Catfish where forbidden food Jews as they don't have any scales. Despite the ancient Jewish laws, we agreed that no one in their right mind would ever want to eat such a slimy, obscene looking fish anyway! The thought of making a meal of it made us pull faces at each other with shouts of "eeeeew!"

It was Sarah who said that we should leave it as a gift on the door-step of the home of Jacob the synagogue leader in the village. With a twinkle in her eye and her cheeky smile she said that he was the kind of man who "really deserves a nice gift like this!"

On one of our lazy afternoons lying on the rock I had mentioned to Sarah that once, when I was seven and had recited the Torah slightly wrong, he had picked me up by my ears and thrown me outside in disgust, shouting the very name that then stuck. All the children copied his taunt from that day. I would forever be known as Lame-dog. With stinging ears, I limped home with that curse of being known as nothing but a lame dog.

Sitting waiting for Dad to return, thinking of Sarah and our catfish gift brought a smile to my face. I hadn't smiled since that awful day at the river and the act of smiling felt bad, like I was betraying her. But then again, rotten catfish falling on the head of an angry man when he opened his door was too funny. Someone said that his scream could be heard in Jerusalem! Served the bugger right. The fact that we had never been found out made the prank even more satisfying and our friendship grew even closer.

I emerged from my daydream with my half smile to watch again, eyes fixed on the winding road. Waiting for dad. He would know exactly what to do about the soldier. He was strong.

Once more he didn't come. Not today. But I felt it would be soon. Very soon.

It was ten months and three days of the same routine: helping mum, fetching wood and any food, making some money when I could and then a long wait by the fig tree. Alone. There was no more word about Sarah and she was soon forgotten in the village. But our games, conversations, swimming and fishing replayed in my mind over and over, she was as close to me now in my thoughts as she had always been. There wasn't a single thing which I did that didn't carry the filter of my Sarah in my thinking.

The tree looked like I felt. After months of sitting by it, waiting, I had become almost one with it, and those that passed didn't seem to see me merged into the shape of the tree. It held my burdens as I leant back on the weathered bark. The colour of the trunk was different where I had sat, a lighter shade the shape of my back where I waited. Alone. I even spent my thirteenth birthday there, alone. Mum had forgotten and hadn't been able to rise from her prison of bed on that day. I was alone then as I was for most of that year. Waiting.

The tree leaned comically, too low on its side away from the road, as if it, too, was just about to give up but somehow held on with some sliver of hope. Its limbs gave the impression that it required too much effort to reach up and stay clear off the dusty ground where it precariously leant, and the branches held the tree up as if supporting it by its knuckles and knees. In its prime it must have been manna from heaven for the local children at harvest time – the low hanging fruit made it easy for them to fill their bags for a feast. But now only a few figs were growing, small and hard. Not-yet-ripe fruit on an old worn out tree. They looked out of place, like they were trying too hard to grow. I rested my back once more and looked. On this day I looked up and breathed the prayer that was like an ache in my body, 'God, if you are there, please bring my dad to me today...'

Before I could even utter my 'amen', I was captured by the distant silhouetted figure walking up towards the village. The sun was behind him, but with my heart racing I knew it must be Dad. Jumping off the wall, I shouted, 'Dad is that you?' and shuffled my way towards the approaching figure. He had the same build as him, the same long cloak. I held my breath.

The man had long tangled hair and a short beard and was carrying an old worn leather bag with a blue cloak poking out from the top. It wasn't him. He broke his stride to step around me and then stopped.

"I'm looking for Philip, son of Joseph, the son of Hezekiah," he said solemnly.

He looked above me, not in my eyes. Awkwardly trying to find an object to focus on, anything but looking at me.

I blurted out, "That's me! I've been waiting for Joseph. He's my dad. Have you any news of him? When is he returning home? I hope you say soon, as Mum has been really sick and something so awful has happened to my friend. She was down by the river and..."

He interrupted me and said, "I haven't got time for this."

And with that phrase I stopped mid flow and held my hands out in front of me, as if pleading for some bread.

"Look, I'm just passing through, boy. I've been given a message and I am on my way home. I worked with you dad."

Panic rose in me and I shouted, "Worked? *Worked*? What do you mean worked with him?" I grabbed the stranger around his wrists and demanded to know. "What's happened?" I shouted firmly with my knuckles turning white holding on to ensure he didn't walk off.

"Calm down, lad, he hasn't died and he's fit and well. It's just that..." The man looked even more uncomfortable and still didn't look at me but rather looked upwards towards the clear blue sky. For a moment I wondered what he was watching so I also looked up, and then he began talking once more.

"He asked me to give this to your mum, Hannah. It's a certificate. They're getting divorced, you see lad. Here, you take it to her."

And with that, he pulled his arms down in one sweeping move, freeing himself from my grasp and reaching for the scroll from his bag. Once he had found it, he threw it at me. It landed at my feet. As I looked down I saw dark spots appear on the ground around it and on the light brown of the dirty, rolled up scroll. It looked strange and for a moment I didn't know where the splattering marks were coming from...

The stranger quickly turned and, now with his back to me, he simply broke back into his stride once more and carried on his journey home. I caught the only two words of farewell under his breath... "Poor bastard," he said as he walked towards his family, shaking his head. No doubt he had gifts in his bag for his children alongside his ample wages.

I was left with the scroll. A certificate of divorce from my dad for my mum. Nothing else. Just the scroll on the ground by my feet. I didn't move until he had gone and all I could see was a distant shape making its way up the far hill.

News of the divorce soon filled the village and the scant information that the stranger had shared with me was soon added to by a 'friend,' someone whom I had never seen call in to see my mum but now had a keen interest in talking. She stood outside the courtyard gate to offer her sympathy as Mum propped herself against the other side. Even in her awful news she remained ostracised by her illness. I heard them talk and sitting quietly in the courtyard I caught everything. Mum asked question after question as to what her friend had heard about Joseph. This is what she found out:

Dad had believed that her time wasn't long and that pouring all his hard-earned cash into paying for the physicians was only prolonging the inevitable. Besides, the landlady in Rome who had offered him board and lodgings as dad waited for the ship's company to negotiate trade back to Dor was now his new wife. One thing led on to another.

"You know how it is, Hannah," Mum's friend gently reassured, "he was never coming back and I don't think he had any intention of doing so, especially as you have been so unwell and it's obvious that you are…" the friend trailed off and through the gate I saw her underneath her cream coloured shawl literally biting her bottom lip stopping herself mid-sentence.

"You are… what?" Mum shouted.

"I didn't' mean anything hurtful, sorry Hannah, it's just that you've been so sick." She replied.

"You were going to say *now that you are dying*, weren't you?" Mum's voice sounded strong and sharp.

The stranger friend bowed her head and whispered her goodbyes and set off, stepping backward with her head bowed low, desperately trying not to catch the fiery blue eyes of my mum.

Mum slumped at the gate with her back to the wall. Eyes closed. I wanted to reach out to her, but she didn't know that I had heard the conversation, so to distract myself I began to tot up the things that we still had that could be sold to support us now that Dad wasn't coming back home. As I did, a wave of despair came over me. Dad hadn't even sent a single mite to help us.

As I looked around the yard it was painfully obvious that all the things of value of Dad's had already been sold to pay for the medicines and care.

There wasn't so much as a trace of his life in our home and there was very little that Mum and I owned together. And now our simple house would be taken away from us, too. We couldn't afford to pay for any upkeep, let alone afford to feed ourselves. For twelve years, Dad had looked after Mum with everything she needed and now it appeared that he had had enough and was leaving her to die. And leaving me. With no-one.

I looked at mum and she still had her eyes closed, only this time she wasn't sleeping out of exhaustion – her lips were moving and, rather strangely, her face shone as the evening sun seemed to focus on the small opening in the wall of the yard and stream through onto her, like shards of light. She looked strangely peaceful. Looking at her glowing cheeks, I thought for a moment that perhaps everything really would be alright. Then I shook my head sharply and snapped myself away from such false hopes. This wasn't a sign. It was just the evening light. There was no God who would help us. We were alone.

As the darkness fell, Mum remained at the wall with her eyes closed. I looked at her for a long while, her lips still gently moving in silent prayer. A weight of responsibility started to ache upon my chest and shoulders. How would I cope? This was never meant to be my role in life. How on earth did my dad think I was going to look after Mum and make enough for the house and food and doctors' bills? Betrayal didn't even come close to describing what he had done to us. It wasn't just a certificate of divorce Dad had sent. It was a death warrant. All my hopes of Dad helping me were now lost and, with mum having no help now to pay for the precious medicine, there was simply no way I could make money to care for her. All the dog crap in the world wasn't enough for me to find a way to pay for the physicians and medical bills.

The burden turned to dark plans. In the quiet of the obscure courtyard, sitting in silence, I began to plot how I would kill the soldier. I had no choice now but to do it alone. Dad wouldn't be coming home to help me, so I would have to kill the soldier alone or at least die trying.

The knife came from Judas the tanner. I dutifully collected another bagful of muck for him, but instead of my usual generous wages I enquired as to whether he had an old knife as payment instead, making the excuse that ours had become too rusty to repair. It was a spare knife that he had used for slicing open the oxen, and the sharp edge flashed for a moment as I examined it under my cloak, crouched behind a rock. I was well hidden, yet the barracks were well within my sight.

The handle was dark brown. Wooden, with three bronze nails running along the middle of it holding the pointed blade in place. Unless you were part of the army it was illegal to carry a knife, and being found with one could result in a severe beating or even prison for a few weeks.

It had taken me a few days to muster the strength to get to where I was now. Positioned behind the rock, my fingers skipped up and down the knife as I caressed it once more. They shook. But that was to be expected. I was determined to see it through, and as I held the knife, gripping it as hard as I could to stop the shaking, it still moved involuntarily as I moved uncontrollably.

The knife had also been used in other ways. To release some of the pain in me and in those desperate dark moments of yearning for Dad's return and missing Sarah, when that woollen blanket of sorrow surrounded me, I had cut a long line on top of my arm and watched the crimson droplets fall to the ground. The drops made a light sound like the beginnings of storm drops on a dusty path. I could see my own inward pain laid out before me in the dust. Like a child's painting. On many occasions I grappled with the thoughts of turning my arm to face the veins and with one quick swipe to run the blade across my wrist. And that would have been it. But it was revenge that kept me alive. I didn't want to waste my lame life for nothing. Why end it when I could finish it in the aim of killing Marcus Aurelius?

So here I was. Waiting. Longing to kill the one who had robbed me of the kind strength I once had in my best friend Sarah. He would pay for it.

I had rehearsed the speech over and over in my mind as I would thrust the knife deep, watching the scum die in front of me. And as I waited I mumbled them under my breath, watching the large wooden gateway. It stood tall, worn with much use where soldiers had opened and closed it, which had created a worn oval hole so that I could see who was going to leave the barracks just before they did. The sun had bleached the wood white and the gate looked strangely out of place with the crudely cut poles that formed the perimeter of the barracks. They still had their dark bark on them and had been shaped to form a rough menacing spike at the top.

The barracks were surprisingly poorly guarded and I contemplated somehow just limping in. Bold as brass and unannounced with a story of needing food and help. However, for now I was grateful for the wait undetected by the rock as the journey there was easily the furthest I had travelled in my lifetime and my legs were screaming out in pain. Peering over the rock at what felt like a stone's throw from the main gate, I ducked down as I saw though the hole some troops marching. The gates noisily opened, accompanied by the filthy banter of soldiers mocking each other.

He wasn't in this group. I was relieved, as I wanted him alone. I knew his strange behaviour of travelling alone would happen again. The soldiers marched on past me, I was invisible to them as I crouched behind the warm grey boulder. They sounded irritated and I heard them talk of crowds and mayhem in Capernaum.

"Why do we have to do this? For one flippin', Rabbi!" shouted a fat, unshaven, red-eyed soldier who reminded me of a pig that had been in the sun too long. Squeaking and complaining. Whining.

"More like some kind of rebellion, I reckon," one of the burly soldiers replied clasping the handle of his sword.

I waited the whole day. The noise of the gate jolted me awake. I quickly adjusted my eyes to the dusk and out wandered the figure of the man I had dreamed of killing every day for nearly a year. I had forgotten how tall he was and his sheer size made me freeze for a moment. It was too late to be paralysed with fear and I adjusted my stance to crouch, ready to kill.

Unlike the first time we had seen him he was fully armed with a sword in his scabbard and a dagger tucked into his belt. His dagger by comparison made mine look like a miniature. But I knew there was no turning back for me and despite my momentary fear I began to hunch behind the rock ready to spring out as best I could.

It was unmistakably him. One ear. Fat stomach. As I watched, it felt almost dreamlike. The timing was almost too perfect and I began to smile. It was as if he had been led to me. I knew without a doubt that I needed to take this God-given opportunity and thinking in this way somehow made me feel much stronger. I glanced down at my hands, the right one clasping the dagger. They were now still and steady. As I watched Marcus, he strode hurriedly opposite to where I hid, across the narrow path trod by the soldiers to three tall pine trees. He took long steps and then, with his back to me ,as he got closer to the trees he hoisted up his short outer garment of red and began to urinate even before he reached the trunk of the middle one.

I stepped closer. The cloak hugging my chest pulsated and its movement caught my eye for a moment and I stood watching the cloak move up and down, up and down, like it had a life of its own. It was as if I could hear my heart pounding and for a split-second I puckered my lips to usher a low 'shhhh' to my heart so that Marcus wouldn't hear it pound.

The white of my knuckles showed through my brown skin as I clasped the blade. A few metres away from him, beads of sweat formed on my brow as I crept close enough to hear the low vibrations of Marcus humming a tune and the sound of him urinating. His one eared head bowed low, concentrating on the business in hand and making sure he didn't wet his outer garment, which he held awkwardly with one hand stretching half way round his body.

A thought flashed through my mind of how I could decapitate his manhood, but then I reasoned that the best bet was to stab him from behind. Unseen, standing in his shadow, my breathing became more pained and, with the dagger held high above my head, I knew that the only chance was right then and there. That I needed to strike him in the back, hard. I stepped to the right so as to strike the blade where there was an ample gap in-between his ill-fitting dirty breastplate. My arm felt stuck above my head with the blade in hand ready to lunge but not moving.

"Philip. Don't. Please," shouted Mum. The strong voice made me turn immediately to see where she was standing and to warn her of the soldier. But she was not there. No-one was. No-one. I quickly glanced behind me as Marcus pulled his tunic down while wiping his hands on it at the same time. It was too late, I needed to get away. Quickly. I tucked the knife inside my cloak out of sight and walked as confidently as I could back into town, away from the man I so desperately wanted to see dead. As I walked away I looked for Mum, wondering how she could have found me and wondering where she was hiding. How had she been able to walk all the way out to the barracks to stop me killing the soldier? She was not by the rock so I strode back along the track.

He called out in a slurred voice as I walked away, "Oi! This is private land. You're trespassing. Don't let me see you around here again you little cripple or I will beat you senseless, you hear me? You hear me Lame-dog?" I checked behind me to make sure he wasn't following, but he had made his way back to the gate, stumbling as he went. He was drunk.

5

My Mum

The sound of the busy brushing in the near-dark of the encroaching night was strange. A lady was busy in the yard, energetically cleaning up, and there were about five tall piles of leaves and dirt dotted around. A small fire flickered in the middle and I paused for a moment, mid-stride, wondering who had lit it. One of the piles she had neatly brushed stood by mum's bedroom door and as I stepped over them I knocked some of the dried leaves off and they danced around the newly brushed smooth yard. In the firelight it looked as if the leaves were chasing one another.

The helper hadn't noticed my mistake as she was so busy in her hard work. I called for mum through the door into the darkness but there was no answer. At my call, the brushing in the yard stopped and the woman looked at me quizzically, now with the broom leaning against her hip and her arms folded in front of her. Feeling sorry that I had caused some of the leaves to abandon the pile I bowed by head low and pointed at the fluttering escapees and politely apologised.

"Sorry about that. But, I'm looking for my mum. I wonder have you seen her, she is usually in her room on her bed... she's not well you see." The woman straightened and placed her right hand on the broom firmly next to her and held it tight and leant on it like a large walking stick. With the other hand she lifted it slowly and beckoned me to come closer to her, but I didn't move. Rather I patiently waited for her to reply. I looked at her blushed face. It was then that the woman said exasperatedly,

"My goodness Philip! Come on, son! You don't even recognise your own mother!"

I looked at the woman once more.

"Mum? But, what are you doing, you're going to make yourself worse!" I shouted.

"Worse?" she laughed. "Look at me, Philip!"

There was no question she looked different. The paleness that had characterised her had gone and instead there was colour in her cheeks. Something that I had never seen. Twelve years of constant bleeding had made her like an empty grey vessel. And now she was before me with the yard properly swept for the first time in years.

Her arms felt good around me and we sat in the middle of the courtyard with me upon her lap, like a small child. "Philip, I prayed you would come home and see me, to see that I had been healed this afternoon. I couldn't find you son. So I prayed that you would come home."

Hearing her speak with my ear pressed against her chest felt soothing, the words reverberated inside her and into me and combined with the embrace I felt something that I had only felt before when Sarah had embraced me and kissed me. Everything was going to be alright.

"You called me home." I gently sobbed. "I heard your voice. I was just about to…" and then all I could do was cry. With each bellow from the pit of my stomach small parts of the heaviness of losing Sarah, of trying to kill the soldier and of Dad not coming home fluttered away like those leaves I had kicked free.

While I sat in Mum's embrace, she explained that it was a travelling Rabbi that afternoon who had healed her. Instantly. I quizzed her about it, especially how he had been able to touch her because of her sickness. Mum explained that she had woken in the afternoon and had just enough strength to lift herself off the bed to see large crowds out on the streets forming just outside our gate on the main road.

"I heard people say that this man had powers and that many had been healed, that eyes had been opened and that people who had been paralysed all their lives had been instantaneously able to walk again. I knew it sounded too good to be true, but I had this hope grow in me and it just wouldn't go away. It was like I started to smell something sweet again, like some roses wafting scent into my heart. It's strange, I just knew something was good about this Rabbi."

I listened and nodded my head for her to go on.

"With the hope increasing in me, I remembered the only bit of the Scriptures that my dad, your grandad, had taught me. I hadn't thought of it for years but it was as if they were re-written upon my forehead and burning into my mind this afternoon. The words are from the last book of the Prophets: 'But to you who fear my name shall the sun of righteousness arise with healing in its wings. You will go out, and leap like calves of the stall.'

Mum stopped. She breathed heavily and holding back the sobs she said. "I mean, look at me Philip, it's like I'm young again!"

I nodded and then shook my head straight after. It was unbelievable. For a frightening moment I thought that I would awake from a beautiful dream and find myself by the barracks again, waiting to kill Marcus. But I didn't wake up, I remained lying on Mum's lap, looking up at her face brimming with energy. Her cheeks shone and there was a smile that I hadn't ever seen before upon her, not a trying-to-smile kind of smile, but rather one that remained. All I had known was weakness in her but now I heard, in a depth of voice that seemed to dance as she spoke, one that I had never heard. She continued her narrative from the afternoon. Her words were soothing, bubbling and animated and I wanted to hear more.

"I knew I needed to touch the edge of his prayer shawl and receive that healing. I waited. Philip you should have seen me, I crouched by the gate on all fours like a cat! When he walked by, people rushed around him asking for help and healing. He then stopped right by our gate when the synagogue ruler from the next town asked him to heal his daughter. It was my chance and on my hands and knees..." She paused as she began to laugh. "Philip, I literally crawled in-between the legs of the crowds and I brushed my fingers at the edge of the tassels." As she said 'brushed my fingers' she playfully brushed my long hair on my forehead.

"I didn't hold on to them, I just brushed them, like a weak wave in-between the tassels on his prayer shawl." Mum waved her hand gently once more through my hair to show what she had done.

"You see, just a brush… no-one could have seen or felt me do it. It was at that very moment a surge of power flowed through my fingers. It was like a wave that intensified through my fingers." She stopped as tears rolled down her cheeks and landed upon my face as I looked up at her.

"Yes, it was a wave of love flowing in me and right on top of me. That very moment I felt the blood dry up and the stabbing pain in the pit of my stomach ceased. It just stopped. Completely. One moment the pain that I had carried every day for twelve years like a knife hanging from my stomach, it just stopped. Right then, as I brushed my fingers on His shawl." Mum was finding it hard to talk as she was crying, but a joyful crying one with that big smile I was mesmerised by.

"It just stopped." She stated again. "It was then that the Rabbi shouted, 'Who touched me!' There were so many people who were crushing and pressing around him that it could have been anyone. It was then that he looked down, right down onto the street and looked at me on my hands and knees and with His eyes that were full of love he looked deep into me, stooped low down and whispered to me: 'Your faith has made you well. Go in peace.'

5. My Mum

"Philip, I've been healed. It's true. I mean just look at me. I am not sick anymore!"

I smiled up at her and saw her eyes fresh and once more I soaked in the beauty of her face, full with colour. She looked beautiful, for where I had only seen dreariness all my life I now saw life. There was no doubt that mum had been made well. No doubt. Yet, I had two thoughts jumble around my mind. I felt so happy, yet confused. How could a Rabbi have done this? Surely stories of God healing anyone were just in ancient times, but not now. As these thoughts were going through my mind mum gently touched my ankle, the one that had never had any feeling, just numbness and as she touched it she whispered, "What I have received I now give to you, I command healing in your ankle right now. In Jesus name!"

I so much wanted to stay still and carry on enjoying the moment, celebrating mum being well but instead I shuffled off her lap. I wasn't too sure why, but at the time it felt too much to be prayed for, and in protest at her prayer I stood up. Her prayer felt weird and also at that moment, as she touched my ankle, I felt strangely dirty. It was only a couple of hours since I had raised a dagger ready to murder a Roman soldier and now my mum was placing her hand upon my lame ankle.

I tried to explain. "Mum, I'm so pleased for you, I really am, but this just feels too much... Look, let's talk more over some food, it's amazing how you have been made well, it truly is. But I'm not sure that this is for me. How about I collect some firewood and we can cook something to celebrate!"

She nodded. "Good idea, son. I agree, it is so much to take in, I mean look at me!"

As I walked out of the old green gate from the yard to search for some more firewood, mum called after me.

"Philip!" she cried with the sound of such joy in her voice that made it sound like she sang my name. I stopped and turned to her waiting to see what it was she wanted.

She pointed down at my feet. "You're not limping."

6

My Rabbi

The blisters hadn't bothered me and having any kind of sensation in my right ankle and foot felt great. Running felt good. So good. I kept looking down at my once lame leg in disbelief, wriggling and moving it around freely. Getting places felt like a blur as it happened in a fraction of the time they used to, and soon my surroundings felt strangely small and confined, when before it was near impossible to walk from one end of the town to the other.

I used to have a recurring dream: I could run and, as I did run, faster and faster, I would float as my feet still moved, eventually in mid-air. I would spiral up and up, like an eagle. Effortless. Upon the thermals that felt like many soft hands. The aching disappointment when I woke, gutted with the realisation that it had just been a dream, used to make me cry. Now I would cry as I really did run. And boy, this lame dog could run, and run fast!

Neighbours shook their heads in disbelief as I sprinted past their homes and the news of Mum and me being healed through the Rabbi brought many people to our door over the weeks with quizzical expressions. Children would come and stare at us and giggle as they saw me jump up and hop around on the once completely lifeless foot! More surprising than the inquisitive visitors were the gifts of bread, cloth, fruit and firewood that each person brought. It was as if our neglect in the village due to Mum's illness that had made her unclean was being redeemed. Our immediate neighbour had even brought two wineskins full of the finest of wines – a vintage from a few years ago.

The noise was hard to get used to. The noise in and around the home. This confused me at first as, for all my life – and I mean *all* my life – all I had known was silence or hushed tones, as mum was always sleeping in bed. Now there was laughter. Lots of it. At first I felt offended by the noise and I nearly snapped at my mum who was laughing with a friend. The words forming on my tongue were 'be quiet, mum is sleeping!' I caught myself before saying it and joined in with the laughter echoing around our open yard. It was absurd and it was good.

The track down to our river eased gently and the slope made me run even faster than before. As I approached, I tried to slow but couldn't. Holding out my hands I took the impact upon the rock that Sarah and I had spent many days upon, daydreaming and playing. Stopping so suddenly brought a sharp pain to the palms of my hands, but this felt strangely pleasing too. They stung, but it wasn't through falling down when they used to take the full force of me as I tripped upon my lame foot. My hands were fine, no blood, and besides – the exhilaration of running far outweighed any pain to my hands. I was still inspecting them, palms open in front of me, when I saw him by the rock.

He was sitting where I had first met Sarah, when we had accidently found each other, she on one side of the rock and I on the other throwing stones into the river. He also was throwing stones, skimming some that then danced upon the water's surface, seemingly floating upon the ripples before diving deep into the coolness.

He had a kind face and his eyes had laughter lines in the corners. They shone, much like when the sun's ray's sparkle off the surface of our river. They, too, seemed to flow and his gaze upon me felt uncomfortable. And yet I didn't want to run or look away.

"Hello, Philip." He gently said.

How did he know my name? I stood looking at him, thinking of what would be a good response to his greeting and working out how I could get away from him as soon as I politely could. I was just about to open my mouth when he held out his hand to me, a ripe fig upon it.

"I heard you under the fig tree, when you were waiting."

"Have you been spying on me? Why were you watching me?" I confronted, taking two steps towards him. I held my arms in front of me, open and questioning.

His gaze didn't change, he just smiled.

The fig looked ripe. As I starred at it I became confused by the illogicality of it being in his hand. It wasn't the season for figs. There were none in the village.

Taking my eyes off the fig I looked directly at him and snarled: "How the heck do you know me? Have we met before? Who the fig are you?"

I wished I had managed to come up with something a little bit more manly and confrontational. He coolly looked down at the fig in his hand and then looked at me, the corners of his mouth turning upwards. He glanced at the fig again and then into my eyes and burst out laughing!

"Who the fig are you?!" he mimicked.

His laughter was contagious and I couldn't help but laugh along with him and as I stood there, belly aching, I joined in the comedy over the fig. It felt like I knew this man well. How could I laugh so long and hard with a complete stranger? It was absurd.

He gently placed the fig on our rock, the one that years before had baked those that I had scrumped from the neighbour's tree.

Still laughing, he said, "My name is Jesus."

With those four words, I was rooted to the spot, unable to move. As he said his name it bounded in me and resonated like an echo, yet stronger, like a gale wind you feel upon your face, but only this was inside me.

"I am the one who healed your mum a few months ago," He said. "And yes, I do know you. I've come searching for you, Philip, as I have something to ask you. I can't bring your dad back home but I need to let you know that there really is a God. He is real and He is like a good dad."

I nodded and asked: "You're 'the' Jesus?" I walked closer to him and as much as I tried not to, as I shook my head in disbelief, tears flowed freely down my cheeks and it was at that moment I felt incredibly known. He held out his hand to shake mine.

"It's so good to meet you properly, Philip," he calmly stated.

"Listen, I need to say something," I blurted.

"Thank you. Thank you for healing my mum, I don't know how you did it, but I am so indebted to you. She had been so unwell, for over twelve years." His gaze didn't change and he simply smiled a cheeky smile.

"It's a real pleasure you know, Philip. It's the reason I'm here. I've been sent to destroy the works of the evil one. You see, the Kingdom of Heaven is closer than you think and what you have seen in your mum is a sign… It shows that God's reign is now here."

We stood in silence and as we did, the gentle flow of the river over the rocks seemed to make a song. It was as if the atmosphere around us was thick with inaudible melodies. And there was a smell, not of old manky river bed but of freshness, it smelt like fresh bread and posh perfume. Each breath that I breathed in of this smell seemed to untangle in me the feelings of rejection and neglect. It was a matter of moments but from walking towards Jesus to holding his hand I felt like I had grown and that my back had straightened. It was as if I had become Philip. Not Lame-dog. He was gone. As these thoughts sprang around my mind and with Jesus still holding my hand, he asked,

"Are you enjoying running with your new foot?"

"Enjoying it? I'm flipping loving it... I run everywhere! If I could I just wouldn't stop! Hang on, how do you know these things?" I asked.

He didn't answer but rather bent down and picked up a stone. He skimmed it well and it bounced upon the surface three times before disappearing back into the river.

I asked again, "How did you hear me at the fig tree? I mean, there really wasn't anyone around and I didn't see you."

He turned to me and indicated that we should sit. To sit upon the very rock that was Sarah's and mine. I wished he hadn't chosen it, the emotions of loss bubbled up again and as we sat he said those very words that Sarah had reassured me a year ago, "Everything will be alright, you know. Come on let's sit and talk."

"I saw you waiting for your Dad, Philip. I'm so sorry he didn't come home, I really am."

I looked at the reeds at the far side of the river and remained silent. They swayed in the breeze, bowing low dipping into the surface of the river and then standing back up again to then repeat the process all over again as if they were thirsty. I felt comforted sitting with him, yet waited for that familiar pain of rejection to rear up deep within me, a sensation that had become part and parcel of me. One that caused me to choke as it tightened around my throat and often caused me to heave and vomit what little food I had eaten.

But, as I waited, the rejection feeling didn't appear. Rather, I felt strangely care-free and that things were all of sudden manageable, even easy. Sitting with this stranger brought a sense of hope in me that I hadn't had before. It was a bit like the times I waited by the tree for Dad, sure that he would come soon, only the feelings were much, much stronger.

Jesus gently explained: "I have been sent by God to bring the lost sheep of Israel to him. People like you, Philip. My role is to show others that God has not forgotten us, he hasn't moved off to never return. He is faithful, he always has enough for us, and sticks close by through thick and thin. He is the one who sees the harm that has been done to people like you and will bring justice. He is also the one who transforms the foulest of this earth, the scum of the earth if you know what I mean. He is good and I am here to tell you that God really is here."

I didn't need to say anything for a while I chose to be still and this didn't seem to bother him in the slightest. I closed my eyes and allowed his words describing what God is like to sink in. Eventually I opened my eyes and watched him balancing some stones on our rock, one upon the other, he had stacked seven and was concentrating on his precarious pile.

"So what do you want from me then?" I asked. He looked up and took his hand off the top stone that then fell and slid off the rock causing the others to fall one by one into the river, each with a satisfying plop.

"Do you want to know God?" he asked looking at me with his river-like eyes again.

"Yes. Yes I think I do." I boldly stated.

"Then, Philip. What I want to ask you is, will you follow me?"

She did a bee-like dance around the yard, erratic and lavish. After she was worn out by her twirling and jumping she let out a loud whoop and shouted praises to God. I must admit that it wasn't quite the reaction I had envisioned when I told her about meeting Jesus down by the river and him asking me to follow him. I wasn't sure how she would take it, but if I was completely honest, her reaction wasn't what I had hoped for. I had hoped that she would have tried to convince me to stay. I bowed my head and looked at the swept yard and wondered why she would be so happy to see me go.

6. My Rabbi

Surely for me to leave home at thirteen was going to be hard for her? My thoughts were quickly interrupted as Mum placed the fig that I had brought from Jesus onto the wooden chopping board and declared, "come on, let's celebrate!"

After she had cut it in two, very purposefully and carefully, as if performing some strange ritual, she placed her hand under my chin and gently guided me so that I would look her squarely in her eyes. As we looked at each other we each held half a fig. Before eating she solemnly held hers in front of her and softly nudged her half into mine as if we held precious goblets of wine making a toast. "To the King!" she declared with a beaming smile and she held her half of the fig above her head.

"The king?" I asked in bewilderment.

"Yes, to King Jesus!" she declared and with that she ate her fig. I copied and shoved my half in my mouth. It tasted good.

I won all the swimming races and was picked first for the team relay. I dreamed of Sarah seeing me win. Closing my eyes I imagined what she would say now and how proud she would be of me. I missed her. My dreams of her became even stronger and more frequent despite the joy of the two weeks of teambuilding, which included lots of eating together. I missed her dearly. Jesus liked food. Each evening before the stories and tales we ate like kings.

He sent us out two-by-two the day after the Sabbath. We were all very different as a band of brothers. The twelve closest to Jesus who had been called first by him were the furthest from 'sorted and together' kinds of guys that you could imagine. They had fights, seemed to question so much of what Jesus taught and often didn't get the training that Jesus brought as he prepared us for our first mission. In a strange kind of way it gave the rest of us permission to be who we were. For many of the others I got to know, they shared that it was the first time in their lives that they didn't need to build up a pretence around who they were. We each had a turn to practice our story of what had happened in our lives and, to be honest, I didn't think mine extraordinary in any way. Until I shared it for the first time around the campfire.

The sparks were dancing above the flames, flying up and up and as I stood and cleared my throat to speak a hush fell upon the band of brothers. I was the youngest in the troop but their attention towards me wasn't as if I was a child in need of indulging but rather one of honour. This was a strange feeling. I felt valued. Held in a high regard and loved by those who had also been called by Jesus.

6. My Rabbi

Despite their kindness, I started to shift from side to side as I moved my weight down on one foot and then the other. I hadn't ever spoken to a group of people before, let alone as big a group as nearly a hundred men. Jesus looked up and winked at me and mouthed some reassuring words: 'You will be fine.'

I stopped swaying and instead held up my head high and opened my mouth to speak. The crowd seemed to hang on to every word that I shared and when I got to the bit about planning to murder the old soldier Marcus because of what he had done to Sarah, I spoke of the very act of committing revenge and how I was supernaturally stopped, it was then that I saw tears on the faces of the men watching me. As I looked around the campfire, the light revealed the sparkling tears. My rescue had truly been a drastic one, and instead of dying at the grand old age of thirteen at the hands of a soldier, I was telling my story as a healed man, one who had been called to change the world and announce that the Kingdom of heaven was near.

Telling our stories was all part of preparing us to go into the surrounding towns and villages, but our training wasn't all about our stories. We were also taught by Jesus every morning, with games or jobs to make the camp useable in the afternoon, followed by a feast and listening to one another's stories in the evening. What he had to share made my head ache but what hurt most were my sides. Jesus did more than teach me about generosity and grace – I also learnt how to laugh. Real belly ache laugh, my stomach seriously hurt from it. I had never giggled so hard and for so long when listening to story after story and hearing some of the encounters that the first friends of Jesus had.

We didn't run much, in fact we didn't run at all together, despite my enthusiastic jogging loops around him, he just steadily plodded on towards our destination and he ignored me for the most part. I had so much nervous energy and anticipation for what we were tasked to do, so in my thinking the sooner we got there the better. Not so with Thomas.

The road was long and straight and apart from the sharp inclines and declines he marched at a ridiculously slow but steady pace. Thomas was far more used to being driven about by horse and cart and at first he struggled with the few hours walk. His ample belly told a story of luxury. Too much wine. Too much fine food. Yet Jesus found it fit to pair us up and as one set of partners among the Seventy Two. We were told to head towards the town of Beth Shean, south of the Sea of Galilee.

The Hare and Tortoise of Jesus' mission.

Our instructions where to greet people whom we met with the familiar greeting of peace and we were told that, if we were greeted back with that kind blessing, we should start from there and bring the news of the coming kingdom and show the power of the kingdom through praying for those who were sick. I was slightly nervous about talking about the kingdom and Jesus. But it was the praying that completely terrified me. I couldn't quite work out how the healing thing worked, and besides, a question weighed heavy upon me: what if 'it' didn't happen? What would I do when I offered to pray for someone to be healed and they weren't. What would I do then?

The only healing that I had actually done was when practicing with Matthew, one of the twelve. Part of our training was in smaller groups of seven – including one of those who were first called by Jesus as our instructor. They were fairly new to the experience themselves and had only two mission trips under their belts, but had the advantage of watching Jesus perform many miracles first hand. All of these we had learned about: the calming of the storms, multiplying bread and fish, the paralysed able to walk. Each one of us had also received healing of some sort or other and, as part of our preparation time, I had asked Matthew about his. With the widest grin, he declared:

"Jesus healed me from my love of money! When I first encountered him, I was filthy rich… beyond filthy rich! I had everything that I could ever have wanted, my home was full of the most beautiful furniture and treasures, and I had servants, livestock and even owned a large vineyard out towards Caesarea." He lowered his tone, "I could have had any girl I wanted, any night. But I was deeply unhappy. It was only Jesus who saw this. He knew."

"But what did you do with all your stuff?" I asked.

"I gave it all away. Every single bit of it." He laughed. "You see, my wealth was built upon cheating others through the taxes I collected for Antipas and the Romans. I took a bit for them and a little bit for me and over the years the little bits I collected amounted to a considerable wealth. Lots of little bits make a lot of cash. But you know what? I gave back four times the amount I owed people and that left me with nothing. Zilch! And Philip, I have never been happier in my life. Money simply is not in my thoughts and desires anymore. Once it consumed me. The weight upon me thinking about it all the time has been lifted."

He drew close to me and whispered, "Philip, remember that the signs of the coming kingdom may be under the surface where no one can see. If Jesus hadn't healed me of the deep pain I was carrying through my love of money, I reckon I would be dead. Dead. Either through drink or I would have just topped myself." He made a gesture with his hand from one side of his neck to the other and stuck out his tongue and made a gurgling sound.

"He is my saviour. Like you, Philip, I now have a purpose and for the first time in my life I can honestly say that I am happy." And with that he leant back and laughed and laughed some more.

He took me to the far end of the camp to one of the new recruits, an older man who spent most of his time leaning against the trunk of a majestic old Oak at the edge of where the teaching sessions took place. His face was worn and leathered and the rough bark which he was propped up against seemed to merge into his brown face. When we approached him he was sleeping. He looked so peaceful and we stood for some time enjoying looking at the radiance that shimmered over his face. This sleeping elderly man in the shade of the mighty Oak had joy written all over him. Matthew gently shook his shoulder and as he woke he fixed his eyes upon me, they shone with his encounter of Jesus and he gently said, "Arh, here's the young man who will heal these knees."

Andrew had been unable to walk all his life, until his involuntary encounter with Jesus. Four of his friends had lifted him, despite his protests, to the rooftop of an old house where Jesus had been teaching, crowds thick around him and spilling onto the street. His friends had broken through the ceiling above Jesus and, much to Andrew's embarrassment he was lowered down to Jesus, shouting at his friends and cursing them all the while for what they were doing. The story had been told around the camp fire and had caused much hilarity amongst the new recruits! With a word he was healed instantly and was able to pick up his mat and walk with his friends back home. But now his knees that were causing him agony. Years upon years of laying on a bed meant that his knees hadn't needed to support any of his weight and a few months in of walking they had swollen up and were badly bruised. Each step was a step of pain. "Go on..." Matthew placed his hand in the small of my back and gently pushed me towards Andrew.

I stammered, "Right, this is my first time I'm going to pray for healing Andrew so bear with me." and with that I knelt before him.

He just smiled and waited patiently for me to begin. I closed my eyes and blindly reached my hand in the general direction of the swollen blue and black knees. Matthew tapped me twice on my shoulder and I looked round. "Keep your eyes open brother, remember?" he gently instructed.

Despite the pain he was in, Andrew was chuckling as he watched me. At least he was having a good time, I reasoned, and with my heart pounding I quickly announced my prayer with my eyes open, not sure where to look: "I command your knees to be healed in the name of Jesus! All swelling and pain go right now and may your knees, Andrew, may they be made new...and...ummm, amen." Mathew and Andrew said a confident Amen to my faltering one. I stood and made some kind of apology and hurriedly spoke about how prayers for healing could take time.

"Philip." Andrew gently said without moving look at my knees. "The pain has gone."

"Really?!" I asked.

"Really, the pain has completely vanished." He stood as to prove his point and gave me a big hug. Leaning down to inspect his knees, I saw no more swelling and the blue and black bruising had turned to a light yellow and greenish colour.

Remembering all this gave me a renewed confidence as I walked with Thomas on our first mission. Just as well, as our first couple of days of walking were difficult. It didn't help matters that we were told not to take anything with us, no money, and no spare clothes. No-one checked as we left, but we respected our teacher and what he told us we obeyed. On the first night that we were sent out we had greeted people on the way, but no one had wanted to talk and everyone seemed in a rush, heading to the market, visiting loved ones or just plain busy.

We waited by the side of the road in the hope someone would welcome us into their home for the night but, as the evening got colder, Thomas made the decision to wash in the stream and find some shelter for the night by a stone wall and bed down until the morning. It was a warm spot as the stones had soaked in the heat of the sun. I was used to missing meals but judging by the sounds coming from my companion, he wasn't. His belly groaned and gurgled throughout the night.

Thomas didn't say much the second day either, but did make a lot of noise as he walked. Too slowly in my opinion. As we walked I noticed the peculiarities about him. He had much shorter hair than was customary and I didn't quite know how to ask him about it but I knew the unusual characteristic of his hair would make him stand out on our journey and that others may ask him about it.

"So, Thomas, I've been meaning to ask you..."

"About my hair?" he responded sharply and abruptly stopped in the middle of the road and closed his eyes. Quickly he opened them and looked up. "Looks kinda, weird, don't you think?" His hands were on his hips and he took the opportunity to catch his breath from walking.

I was taken aback by his bluntness and blurted out, "No, it's lovely." I was lying, of course. "It's just that I wanted to ask you about why it was so short and whether it may be a new fashion from Rome, perhaps...?" My words trailed off and I felt awkward. But walking with him for two days and having slept next to him by the wall for one night, I felt that I had earned the right to know. I just couldn't stop looking at it as some of the hairs hadn't been cut and they looked strangely out of place sitting proud amongst the shaved ones. Especially when the sunlight caught them and they seemed to bounce up and down with each step he took. It was downright distracting. His freaky appearance was proving too much of an interference for me on our way to our mission, as much as I tried I couldn't focus on the task in hand.

"Come off it Philip, it looks strange and I know it." He smiled at me reassuringly and said, "Why don't we walk and talk?" We did, in silence, and after a while he said: "I was a Qades."

"A what now?" I asked, not having heard the term before.

"Let me explain. I used to be a temple prostitute in the Canaanite religion," he said bluntly. "There, I've said it and if you want to turn back I don't blame you, but I can illuminate what happened in my life if you like..."

I carried on walking, keeping quiet, but unconsciously I widened the gap between us as we walked. We had plenty of time and he didn't skimp on the detail.

Even with the wind blowing against us he spoke steadily. The weather made us slow down our pace considerably as he continued his story. I was grateful in a strange way, as this allowed even more time for Thomas to share.

His short hair wasn't a fashion statement but rather given to him as a symbol of disgrace from his close friends who were also temple prostitutes. He explained that he had given up on his Jewish faith and run away from his parents as a young man and moved away to Corinth, soon after his twin sister had died in an accident when they were twelve years old. He had blamed himself as it was his idea to sneak up onto the roof of an old house, which she had fallen through and never recovered from her injuries. "She died a slow and painful death," Thomas said and shook his almost bald head.

He had needed money and found a job that came with lodging in the temple of Apollos. One job led to another. After a few years he joined the ranks of the temple prostitutes, or 'sacred prostitutes' as they were called. Thomas explained that the Canaanites thought that sacral prostitution was a form of sympathetic magic; as people performed sex acts this stimulated sexual activity among the gods, ensuring the fertility of the soil. Eventually Thomas became very ill and made the decision to leave Corinth and return to find his parents. When he shared his plan with his so-called friends, they shaved his head and beat him badly. "They left me for dead," Thomas stated, and with that he stopped, crouched down and started to cry.

"On my way back, looking for my mum and dad, I heard that they had died. It was then that I met a man on the road who called me to follow him. It was so bizarre, like he knew me inside and out." Thomas smiled. "Jesus said to me, 'I know who you are and where you have travelled from. Come and follow me, as I have a good plan for you.' And the rest is what you know. I joined this group and here I am. I haven't looked back, it's been the best couple of months of my life. It's like all the shattered pieces from my life have been put together once more."

We eventually arrived at Beth Shear. At the edge of the town was a small hamlet of homes. "I have a hunch we should call at the middle one, the one with the blue door," Thomas said confidently. We approached the doors and called out to ask if anyone was there.

"What do you two scruff merchants want, hey?" asked a large man who made Thomas look like a twig in comparison. The man's voice didn't match his appearance and while he appeared as tall as he was wide his voice was very high and it was hard to hold back the giggles at the mismatch of his appearance with how he sounded.

"Hello there young boy, is your mum or dad at home?" Thomas said jokingly. The silence was awkward and the large man looked up and down at me and then also Thomas and then burst out laughing. His high pitched guffaw made us laugh uncontrollably too.

"Very funny," he said. "Now what do you want, seriously? I'm busy and I can't stand about all day."

"Well, first off," said Thomas, "I need to say to you "Peace be with you." And with that the large man stood still and for a split second closed his eyes and gently shook his head as if receiving something soothing upon the top of it. When he opened his eyes he looked beyond us.

"Wow, that felt weird," he said. "Well, peace be with you too. Now, why don't you come on in and let me get you a drink and you can explain why you strangers are traveling around these parts. You do look a sight, you know, not carrying any bags or a change of clothes."

The big man left us in the shade of the warm, well-kept yard. In the corner was a beautiful twisting peach tree that wound up and around the whitewashed yard.

He brought some goblets with water as well as a jug full of sweet wine and placed it at our feet and without uttering a word he went back inside to return with a bowl full of scented water and a towel.

"Please," he said. "Sit down, make yourself at home." As soon as we had taken our place on the blue and white woven mat, he reached out to remove the sandals from my feet. "Hey, you don't need to do that, I'm just fine," I protested. But without a word he had already manoeuvred my right foot above the bowl and he tenderly washed the dust and dirt from first my left and then my right foot. After he had washed mine, he changed the water and washed Thomas', the experience of which didn't seem to perturb him in the slightest.

"I see you two are men of integrity." The big man stated. "Now, what have you got to say to me?"

Thomas spoke first, which I was pleased about, as being asked such a question in a training session or with your neighbours seemed natural, but by a complete stranger it just felt weird.

"Is your name Shimon? But your friends call you Simon?"

He nodded. This revelation just didn't seem to faze him.

"Well, you know Shimon means 'to hear', right?" Again he nodded. "Well, what you are about to hear will change your life like it has changed ours." Shimon placed the towel and bowl on the elegant mat and sat cross-legged in front of us, attentive to what Thomas had to say.

"We follow Jesus," Thomas continued, "who has been sent by God to show the lost sheep of Israel what God is truly like and to announce that his kingdom is near." Thomas went on to explain how he had been rescued by Jesus, called and forgiven and brought into a life of purpose.

"And what about you, brother?" Shimon asked nodding towards me.

After introducing myself properly and thanking him for washing my feet I shared my story and when I got to the bit about my mum healing my ankle in the name of Jesus, he asked me to stand and show him how I could walk.

As I walked around his yard explaining the mystery of what had happened, a stabbing sensation went down from my right hip and shot down to the bottom of my foot. It was so sudden that I stopped mid-sentence and simply looked at Shimon and asked, "Have you got pain in your right leg, shooting down the leg into the sole of your foot?"

He nodded and looked unsurprised as to how I could have known about his condition, but then tears started to fall down his cheeks and he bowed low and with a howl he said, "It's so painful! I've had it for months. I've had to stop working and I've started drinking heavily to dull the pain. What are you going to do?"

And with that I commanded the pain to go in the name of Jesus. And as I did so, he started moving and seething around on the floor, letting out a piercing scream. The noise made me jump back and I banged my head upon one of the lower hanging branches of the peach tree.

"It's alright," Thomas reassured me. "You haven't seen this before, Philip, but something similar happened to me when Jesus met with me and prayed for me." And with that Thomas gently reached out his hand and commanded, "Pain get out, peace come in." Shimon relaxed and a shimmer of light fell over his face and his cheeks looked shiny.

Shimon explained what had happened as I started to pray and how he had felt out of control, almost like a battle that was going on for his very life. The pain had gone, but not only did he feel better within himself, there was more. He told us about a careful plan that he had made to end his life that evening. "Look," he said, "I've got everything I need to have finished it." He had a small brown bottle of poison and some strange powder wrapped in a grey piece of leather. He explained that he had bought it for a large sum of money from a man in the market under the pretence that he needed to poison some of the wild dogs in the neighbourhood that had bitten village children. The battle for Shimon's life now made sense. No wonder there had been such a strange struggle. This man was on a road to death, but had now entered into life.

We spoke for most of the afternoon and Shimon asked if we would be willing to stay, as the following day he wanted to invite some of his friends and family to listen to our story of Jesus and what he had done. "It's going to be painful." He announced. "No one knew how desperate I had become and when they find out about my plan to kill myself they may be angry with me." He thought for a while and then declared: "It's a miracle, you know. God sent you to rescue me and show me a new life!"

It started to get dark and, while Shimon busied himself in making a fire and preparing the beds, I noticed he had made up three extra places to sleep, not two. Thinking it slightly strange, I reasoned that he must have been expecting a relative to stay. Just as I was thinking about this he turned to me and said, "Guys, shall we ask your soldier companion to come in now? He must be thirsty and hungry standing guard at the gate in the sun all day."

"Soldier?" Thomas and I asked in unison.

"Oh, sorry. Is he not a soldier?" Shimon retorted, "Then why is he dressed in that golden armoury and carrying that sword? I didn't notice him at first when you arrived, but as soon as you started speaking he stepped into view and I knew that he was there to guard you both and that you two must be very important visitors. Which of course you are!"

Thomas and I belly laughed for an age. We were in awe of what the Lord had done and how we were led to Shimon's house. Shimon didn't quite get why we were so overwhelmed by his question about the soldier until he looked outside and saw no-one standing there.

That evening, as the flames of the fire glowed in the middle of the yard, he threw the packet of powder and the bottle of poison into them. "Don't breathe in for a little bit..." he said as smoke billowed up from the flames.

The following two weeks Thomas and I were under the hospitality of Shimon and we had a steady flow of visitors. The story of Shimon's suicide plan and dramatic healing brought even the most sceptical to his door. Having been so nervous about putting into practice the words about the kingdom of heaven being near, I was blown away by the power that Jesus had granted us. Much to our amazement, Shimon took the risk of even allowing a man who had leprosy into his home, where we prayed and prayed some more for him. But nothing happened. It was only two days later that a man who we could barely recognise came to show us how he had been cleansed.

A fortnight of nonstop praying and talking was beginning to take its toll and despite the exhilaration, I was getting tired.

Early one afternoon I made my excuses and went to seek some solitude and rest inside Shimon's home. Besides, it wasn't just me and Thomas who were able to pray for the sick now, and it was important to let the others take a lead as part of their training too in their new found faith and experience of the kindness of God.

I must have drifted off soon after I had slipped away from the hubbub of the yard to rest, as the next thing I knew I was being shaken by Shimon. As much as he tried to be gentle his sheer size meant it was a startling wake up call for me and I felt like a rag-doll in his grasp!

"Sorry to wake you Philip," he said in his gentle, high-pitched tone. "It's just there's someone asking for you."

"Let Thomas deal with it, would you…. I'm so tired." I protested sleepily.

"She said that she knows you."

"She?" I asked. "What's her name?" I sat upright grabbing at my clothes with my heart pounding.

"Her name? Sarah."

7

My Sarah

AD 28, 14 years old

We stopped walking, it was dark and our path was blocked by a fast-flowing stream. I smiled as we stood on the edge. The water was cold and, as I dipped my toes, I thought that it was as if we were destined to be drawn to living water. Here we were once more.

"You became my best friend by that river. And here we are again by one," she gently said. It was hard to hear her with the noise of the flow over the rocks, so I stepped closer and we stood side by side, our arms touching. The moon was full and for a long moment with our words dried up we allowed the burble of the water to soothe and lull us like we so often used to. There wasn't any awkwardness in the silence and standing with Sarah perpetuated the beauty of the noise of running water. The river felt like it was flowing by our feet but also through us.

She hadn't changed. Other than she looked much more like a woman and less like the girl I knew. She also looked tired and every now and again her eyes would dart to look around her. It was her eyes that made her look different. They seemed cloudier. When we used to play they glimmered with a care-free cheekiness that sparkled, and I would always see joy radiating from her beautiful dark brown eyes. But not now.

The last time we were together at our river was full of pain and anguish. Sarah wasn't able to communicate with me then.

We carried on talking, accompanied by the sound of the playful melody of the river skipping its way over the rocks. Despite the length of time that we hadn't seen one another we easily picked up from where we had left off, talking of swimming games, other children in the village and fishing. I spoke to her about being chosen in the relays and explained every detail about winning the races and my new foot and what Jesus had done for me. With each amazing story that I shared she whooped and clapped. The dull ache of missing my best friend that I had carried lifted, wave after wave, with each enthusiastic response to the stories I shared with her. She laughed at my tales and the more I told, the longer she laughed.

The rock beside us was big enough for both of us to sit side by side, and I pointed to it and took a seat and patted next to me for her to join me. Instead, she stood in front of me. Looking into her eyes, face to face, helped me to share some of the painful stories as well, and I shared honestly about waiting for my dad to help me and how he hadn't returned. I spoke about how God had rescued me within a split second before I went to kill 'that soldier'. It was then that she grasped my hand and leaned forward.

"Philip, did you really go to kill him because of what he did to me? Why?"

I wanted to say: 'because I love you', but the words were stuck in my throat and besides, having my hand held by her caused my head to spin for a moment. It felt so safe, so homely, and these emotions overwhelmed my capacity to speak. Rather than explaining, I sat wishing that the moment of having my hand held by her would last forever. She began to tenderly stroke my hand with her thumb, still looking into my eyes, waiting for an answer. I felt loved by her as she held my hand. I wanted this moment to last forever. If I only had one thing that I could choose to do for the rest of my life I would have chosen to hold her hand. This moment felt like home.

She waited for me to answer and eventually I opened my mouth and said, "You are my only true friend Sarah. You know what? I would die for you. I mean, who else has stuck by me and helped me like you? I went to kill that bastard because he took you away from me. But God saved me from killing him. I would have ended up dead myself."

She didn't say a word, just kept gently stroking the top of my hand with her thumb. Tears started to fall freely down her cheeks, but she didn't seem embarrassed about it, she just cried and cried as she held my hand.

We stood by Shimon's gate. The night was cold and she began to shiver. I held her for a moment and rubbed her shoulders to warm her up. She smiled. Light shone through the dullness of her eyes and this made me smile too. We arranged to meet the next day.

"Philip, can I learn more about Jesus and what he has taught you? Am I allowed to learn about him?" Her question caught me by surprise.

"What do you mean?" I laughed, wondering why she wouldn't be allowed to learn about Jesus.

"Well, first off and to state the obvious: I am a woman. Secondly, I am not a pure-bred Jew like you Philip. So, in other words can an un-Kosher Samaritan who is a woman also follow this Jesus you have told me about?"

I suppose I hadn't considered who could be in or out of this heavenly revolution Jesus had started, and whether someone like Sarah would be permitted to follow him. Her question just didn't seem to match my experience of Jesus and watching those he called and who worked alongside him. Not once had I ever seen him turn someone away. Ever.

"Sarah, I believe if Jesus was standing right here he would say three simple words to you."

I leant forward and with my lips touching her ear I whispered: "Come. Follow. Me."

She turned her head slightly from my whisper and our lips touched and while they were still gently together she whispered, "Good. That is so good."

———————————

She was staying with her aunt and in exchange for her lodging and food she helped with her business. Her aunt was a seamstress and had made the dress Sarah used to wear, the one with the beautiful embroidered flower that I had loved so much. Sarah was hoping that her stay in Beth Shean would teach her a trade to take back to her home town.

We arranged to meet the following evening for a meal with Shimon and Thomas. I wanted her to hear Thomas' story of encountering Jesus and Sarah was keen to listen. His story of rescue from his painful plan to end his life had spread around the region and it was this gossip that Sarah had heard in the market, and that in turn had brought her to me.

"When they described the two travellers who had met Shimon, I knew one of them was you. Don't ask me how. I just knew. That's why I came straight away to Shimon's house and asked for you."

Sarah and I spent a further two months in Beth Shean. Two blissful months. Thomas and I had a regular schedule of prayer for healing and most evenings we would teach and pray with those who wanted to gather around the fire in the courtyard.

Sarah and I met on most days during the warmest times, like we used to back home, and after a few days of meeting up we found a great place to swim, away from the crowds and business of bringing the news of the kingdom of heaven. These times alone with her were recreating times for me and I longed for them more and more. Not just for the solitude and rest, but also because Sarah was simply beautiful. I was intrigued by her and I longed to see her more and more. The few times I manged to steal a glance at her while we skinny-dipped brought an intense longing in me. It was as if warmth rose deeply within. My chest pounded. It wasn't just a desire for intimacy, but rather an overwhelming one to protect her and treasure her beauty.

Our growing friendship held something that was brand new to me. It was a feeling that I had been robbed of all my life growing up, but when I was with Sarah I was able to be truly vulnerable, totally accepted and liked for who I was.

This feeling of affirmation she had lavished upon me from the first day we met, and it was growing the more time we spent together. It was as if she had always known me for who I truly was, but also who I would become. However, with my newly healed ankle I could see that it smarted when I beat her in our swimming races!

It transpired that Sarah's engagement to her older cousin had been broken off after the news of the attack by our river. She had moved back in with her mum and dad, but the way they treated her was appalling. They couldn't come to terms with what had happened and rather than helping her through the ordeal they simply ignored her. As if she didn't exist. Weeks would pass and neither Sarah's mum nor dad would speak to her. Sarah joked and said, "I think I may have been better off married to my old wrinkly git of a cousin with his crappy vineyard in Sebastia!"

For now, her aunt was thrilled with the help Sarah brought and she offered her permanent board and lodgings, for as long as she was able to stay. Sarah's skills in making garments were improving so much that her aunt was able to expand her business – Sarah had made a little money too.

Passover was in a week's time and Thomas and I knew we would be expected back in Capernaum with the first friends of Jesus and the growing band of followers in good time to celebrate it. We would also give our feedback with the others about what we had encountered on our first mission sent out as part of the Seventy Two.

One late evening, Thomas sat down with me to pray, just the two of us. We gave thanks for those we had seen healed and for those who had encountered the closeness of Father God as we spoke about his kingdom being near.

After prayer he said to me, "Philip, I'm going to travel back in good time for the Passover. It's time to move on. I know you have spent some good time with Sarah. She would make a good wife you for, you know. I understand if you choose to stay here. I can explain to the others what has happened. You could even continue the work in praying and sharing the message of Jesus right here."

I turned red at the mention of marriage. Yet the thought of staying seemed right. While there was no way I was ready to get married, I simply didn't know whether Sarah would be happy to be married to someone like me or not. I didn't own a single thing of value. No animals, home or land. Mum didn't have two coins to rub together either and, now Dad had gone, the measure of my wealth was, well, nothing. Zilch. Who would want to marry a poor man like me? Yet the proposal of staying to keep close to Sarah and to spend time with her was very attractive.

I resolved with Thomas that I would talk with her the following day and also ask Shimon if I could continue to stay in his home and welcome people for prayer. His home felt tangibly peaceful and the idea of leaving the very place where we had seen wave after wave of God's presence fall upon and bring life to the most desperate of people just saddened me. It was decided. I would stay and Thomas could go back and join the followers.

I couldn't sleep for most of the night, excited about the prospect of continuing the mission in Beth Shean, and terrified about how to tell Sarah how I felt about her. I drifted off. Eventually. Only to wake suddenly from a vivid dream where I was reading a poem to her about my love. For the first time in my life, I decided there and then to write a poem. It was dark, but I knew Thomas had newly-acquired parchment and ink, his trusty white and blue quill standing by his bedside in a worn leather bag that Shimon had given him. It was easy to locate. The loud snoring was my beacon.

Even though my handwriting was barely readable, I took the rest of the night to write the poem out. It would be worth every missing moment of sleep. Each word I carefully wrote I hoped would do the job of passing on how I was feeling. I really didn't have the ability to speak to her face-to-face about how I felt, and when I finished it I felt relieved.

The following day, while Thomas packed his things and folded away his bed, Sarah and I met. The peach tree where we sat had some handsome fruit on it and Shimon insisted that Thomas should take as much as he could carry. Shimon had already furnished him with loaves of bread, dried fruits and artichoke hearts in olive oil left over from the previous night's meal. Observing Thomas preparing his departure while sitting with Sarah, I was struck by the stark contrast between now and when we arrived at the village looking for the person of peace with whom to share the news. We had arrived with nothing and now Thomas was leaving laden with food and gifts from Shimon.

I began to explain the plan that Thomas had suggested to me, withholding the bit about marriage. I explained how I would seek to live in the village and continue the times of healing and prayer based at Shimon's.

"It would be great to spend more time with you Sarah," I gently added.

And with that I passed the worn parchment to her, delicately rolled up with a dark red cord holding it together. "I can read it to you if you like, my handwriting is so messy," I falteringly suggested, unsure that I would be able to. Sarah held it in one hand and in the other she held some folded cloth with a bright blue twine beautifully tied around it.

"This is your going-away present, Philip," she said calmly. Her eyes, while holding some sadness, seemed to shine at the same time. I simply looked at them, unable to say a word. I began to feel that old, familiar cloak of rejection placed upon my shoulders and heart. But then she spoke once more.

"Last night as I slept, Jesus visited me in a dream," she said. "Man, he's so good. Isn't he? I mean, so beautifully good!"

She was now beaming and through the tears forming in my eyes I saw hers sparkle and shine once more. She continued to recount her dream.

"He told me that you would be going today, and that you were called by him to be a fisherman."

"A fisherman?" I responded, rather stunned.

"Yes, but not like you may think," she explained.

"He said that you would fish for people and that many, many people would encounter fullness of life because of what you will do. He spoke to me of a plan that would bring new life to this world, and while I didn't quite understand what he meant, it felt so good. Philip, the feeling of being deeply loved was just overwhelming." She beamed.

"Go on, open it up," she gently encouraged me, looking at the gift of the folded cloth sitting on my lap.

The outer garment was cream white with a green and brown embroidered emblem of a small fish upon the front. The seams had the same green colour around the edges. It was the most beautiful piece of clothing I had ever seen.

"I got up from my dream and worked through the night to make it for you, I hope you like it," she said as I nodded and tried to smile, torn by the overwhelming sense of sorrow – but also filled with wonder that Jesus had come to speak so clearly to Sarah.

"Go on," she gently said, "Go and change this world for Jesus. We will meet again. Soon. I promise."

I wanted to say something back but I couldn't. I stood, ready to stop Thomas in his departure and to grab the few things I had accumulated while staying with Shimon. I looked at Sarah and simply nodded and tried to smile.

"Oh, and one last thing before you go..." She stood and looked me straight in the eyes and, without even blinking she said, "I love you, too." As she said those beautiful words she gently waved the unread rolled parchment in her hand. And with that she wrapped her strong arms around me and kissed me. My tears flowed over our lips together, but it didn't stop her kissing me more.

Thomas was already at the gate saying his farewells again. Like me, he was amazed by the dream that Sarah had in the night and how Jesus had spoken to her. Sarah stood by, confirming what had happened. He waited as I ran back into the house to gather my things and to bid farewell to Shimon and grab the few meagre possessions I had accumulated while living with him over the past few months. As well as a beautiful new outer garment from Sarah, I had been given a collection of knick-knacks as tokens of thanks from some of those who had been healed. A broken gold brooch, a few old handkerchiefs that had seen better days, a carved wooden spoon and a shepherd's crook which I particularly liked.

I clumsily hugged Sarah once more, carrying as many of my belongings under one arm as I could, and embracing her with the other. Shimon loaded me with as many peaches I could carry and laughed as he waved goodbye, watching me drop some as I walked, bending over and picking them up and then repeating the process until Thomas and I were out of sight.

As Thomas and I started our days walk all I could think about were two things: that kiss and how on earth Sarah had known about my poem.

This is what I had written for her:

My Sarah (a poem by Philip)

I've met a friend for life, I know
You stick by me and will never go
Like all the others that have caused me pain
You are a true friend, constant, comforting like the cooling rain
What I really want to say, every time we are together...

We have laughed so much until we've cried
We know each other out and inside
You are my joy and being known by you
Makes me complete, strong and true
What I really want to say, every time we are together...

I'm going to be your friend for ever
I hope to be your Philip and you my Sarah
There are three words that I've just longed to speak
And now I will write them instead, as I feel weak
What I really want to say, every time we are together...
I love you and will forever.

8

My Journey

We had peaches for dinner, with some of Shimon's delicious bread. We watched the sunset, and while it should have been bliss, my thoughts were with Sarah. I felt strangely lost without her. I wished I could have said more. The following night the menu was the same, apart from the bread, which was like the journey back. Rock hard. Even with the stories of healing and Thomas speaking of the beautiful outpouring of peace that had fallen upon us time and time again as we were obedient to do what Jesus had instructed us, I missed her and it hurt. I tried to laugh and rejoice with what Thomas enthused about, but there was a constant pain. An ache in my chest.

The camp was deserted. There weren't any of the tell-tale signs that the followers had been there. It had been abandoned for some time now. The fire pit was cold, blackened logs around the edges. We had left the camp some months previously with it full of hubbub, laughter and nervous expectation as each pair was prayed for and commissioned to go. To return to the emptiness and quiet was eerie.

Thomas asked around the nearest houses for news about the disciples while I sat beside the unlit fire, drawing charcoal patterns on the abandoned rocks where once the disciples had sat and shared stories. Thomas returned with the news that they had made their way to Jerusalem, but we were warned to be careful, as there had been upset among the well-respected Pharisees and the religious leaders about some of the teachings of Jesus. '

"He even broke the Sabbath rules," one man uttered in disgust to Thomas, explaining that Jesus had seemingly created a new hand for a man who had a withered one.

"Gosh, how awful," Thomas said sarcastically, as he retold the story.

Capernaum to Jerusalem was a good three days' walk – and that was if we kept a good marching pace. We had a choice: if we left immediately, we would be able to get there on the day of the Passover and be in time to celebrate it with Jesus and some of the other followers. Or, we could wait until afterwards and find a home that would welcome us in. The latter idea didn't seem daunting to us, since finding our person of peace in Shimon. We were quite excited about the prospect of finding a new place to stay to see what God would do through us. However, after talking it through, Thomas had a hunch that we should follow in the footsteps of the band of brothers to Jerusalem and we were both champing at the bit to share the exciting news of what we had seen and done in Beth Shean. So, we started on our long walk.

We were used to walking in silence, and our friendship meant that forced chit-chat really wasn't necessary, so what Thomas said out of the blue as we trudged towards the holy city felt deeply significant. "This year's Passover party is going to be a momentous one Philip, I feel it in my bones."

Thomas' pace had improved. Despite being well looked-after by our host in Beth Shean, he had become trimmer and much quicker on his feet, so much so, that every now and again I would do a little jog just to keep up. We decided to take the detour around the top of Lake Galilee and from Bethsaida we would follow the path with the lake on our right and then pick up the trade route along the River Jordan. The route was my idea. I liked the idea of walking along the river with the chance of an occasional dip. This made the idea of the journey manageable to me, especially if we were going to walk in excess of twenty miles each day.

Our confident greetings of peace were not reciprocated, and after Thomas had taken the lead on greeting people in the dusk, I asked if I could have a go. The man we met walking towards us was obviously in a hurry. He walked with a long shepherd's walking stick to aid him and had a weathered, wrinkly, kind face. As he drew near I said, "Good evening, the peace of the Lord be with you." Without breaking stride, he didn't even look up and hurried past.

"Yeah, whatever," he stated flatly.

It was then that we both decided, feeling somewhat downtrodden, to find shelter by a tree and get some sleep, washing first in a small brook that flowed down to the Sea of Galilee. So our first night of the journey was literally under the stars, which sounds magical but the clear skies meant it was bitterly cold. Both of us found it hard to sleep.

I closed my eyes and covered my head with the garment that Sarah had made, hoping that the following day would be better – which wouldn't have been hard, as I had found the day immensely difficult. There was a weight upon me that didn't sit well, a dull ache. Missing Sarah. I wished I had stayed.

We walked in silence for most of the next morning. The stale bread tasted good when we got up, especially as we hadn't eaten the night before. We had reached the River Jordan by mid-morning and the soothing sounds of the river calmed my anxiousness and longing for Sarah. Thomas must have noticed my heartache and, as we walked, he gently prayed for the Lord to strengthen me.

Tomorrow, we would be celebrating the Passover meal and the idea of seeing Jesus again made me smile. I had so much to tell him, especially about Sarah and how she had learnt his teachings from me and had wanted to follow him too as her Rabbi.

Later that afternoon, we stopped by the river. The swim was only to be a quick one, but boy, it was refreshing. Thomas, who had never learnt to swim as a child, paddled his feet while resting upon a worn, smooth brown rock at the river's edge while humming the tune of an old Psalm. Waist deep in the water, I called out, "Thomas! What's that song you're humming? What are the words, I want to hear them!" Without a moment's hesitation Thomas looked up and sang in his low tones that seemed to harmonise with the river flowing over the rocks. It sounded good. He sang a melody, and as he did, I felt compelled to raise my hands in praise. It was a good song and I closed my eyes to drink in the words.

*Sing to the L*ORD *a new song!*
*Sing to the L*ORD*, all the earth!*
*Sing to the L*ORD*! Praise his name!*
*Day after day announce that the L*ORD *saves his*
people.
Tell people about his glory.
Tell all the nations about his miracles.

*The L*ORD *is great! He should be highly praised.*
He should be feared more than all other gods
because all the gods of the nations are idols.
*The L*ORD *made the heavens.*
Splendor and majesty are in his presence.

His song was interrupted by shouting from a group of boys further down the river's edge, standing by a ruin of a grey stone shepherd's hut. They were all around my age, but one of the boys was much taller than the others and he was wildly kicking out at another. His behaviour seemed manic, his limbs whirling one way and then the other as his friends tried to hold him back from hurting the smaller boy trying to defend himself from the flurry of blows and kicks by holding his arms up to defend his face. He shook loose of his friends and chased the smaller boy, who was running as quickly away from him as his legs could carry, closer towards us. He tripped, fell, and the taller boy took his opportunity. Without breaking stride, he ran and kicked the boy in the side of his head. The thud was awful. The smaller boy lay on the ground unconscious, while the older boy rallied into him with kick after kick to his head and side.

Thomas rushed towards them to confront the boy with a shout, but this only angered him further and with one punch to the side of Thomas' head he reeled back. By now his friends had managed to catch up with the out-of-control boy and as one knelt to tend to his injured friend the other two tried pulling him back, one on each shoulder, wrapping their arms around his chest as he writhed. They succeeded in stopping him hurting Thomas further as he sat on the ground, bewildered and undefended from the legs that kicked out frantically, trying to connect with his head. It was then, still standing naked and waist deep in the water, I shouted with all my might: "No! Stop this right now and calm down!"

His head turned and in a sharp motion he fixed his gaze upon me. Without any concern for his clothes or sandals, he broke free from his friends once more and jumped into the water, striding towards me. His eyes looked glazed and his pupils were very small. Despite the manic energy he used to attack Thomas and the boy still lying on the ground, his face was pale. Under his breath I heard him hiss, over and over, with each purposeful stride towards me, "I'm going to kill you, Philip. You will die in the river today."

I wasn't shocked that this young man seemed to know me, and some of the words that Jesus had spoken around the fire one evening on our training rose deep within me, about forcing demons out of people. The fact that he'd used the word 'forcing' now gave me confidence.

I shouted, "Stop, in the name of Jesus!"

He was an arm's length away and had raised his right hand to punch. It hung mid-air and he stood like a statue. I gently told him: "I am going to force you out. Right now, in the name of Jesus. What is your name?"

The young man remained fixed in his pose, hand clenched so tightly that the white of his knuckles bulged through his skin. He opened his mouth slightly as one word was ushered from him: "Anger."

"I command you right now, Anger, to go. Leave this poor boy alone and you are not welcome to come back. You are to go for ever. Now."

And with that he screamed and closed his eyes, suddenly opening them again to look down at what he was standing waist deep in.

"What?!" he shouted. "How did I end up in here?" He began to panic and stumbled on the loose rocks beneath him, sinking into the water. He stood up once more and shouted, "I can't swim!"

I gently reassured him, took his hand and led him safely back to the river bank, where he sat on the rock from which Thomas had, five minutes previously, enjoyed dipping his feet in the river.

Thomas was now standing, very much shaken, but he was able to wash the blood from the side of his face in the river. The other boys had managed to bring their friend round and Thomas, taking one look at the boy who had attacked him, sat bolt upright and stood suddenly, only to collapse once more. His face was a mess and already dark purple and yellow with bruising. His left eye had completely closed over with the swelling.

"What happened?" the tall boy asked, looking at his bloodied feet and hands, shaking them, sucking in air through his teeth as they began to sting. He began to weep as his friends tended to the boy's injuries, and looked around at his friends and the bloody scene. He was bleeding heavily from his side and with Thomas' help they were applying a piece ripped from his cloak as a makeshift bandage. The young man who I had delivered from the evil spirit carried on crying and then spoke so gently I had to step closer towards him as I hurriedly got dressed.

"We had a plan to steal your cloak," he said. "I spied it when you went swimming and it looked valuable. My friend tried to stop me. When he called me a dirty thief, I lost it. I got so angry I remember thinking that I was going to kill him. He's one of my closest friends. How could I have thought such awful things?"

I explained what had happened, step by step, and when I told him about being in the river and how I had commanded 'Anger' to go, he spoke.

"Go? But how did you make it go?"

We spent the afternoon talking and explaining the teachings of Jesus. It was a humbling scene to watch but at the end of our time and with the wounds of the injured boy bandaged, we all sat in a circle and held hands as we took it in turns to say a simple prayer. It was when the injured boy prayed and forgave his attacker that we knew there was a purpose to our long walk to Jerusalem. What would have happened if we hadn't been there?

Spending the afternoon with the boys put us way behind schedule for the Passover celebration in Jerusalem. We needed to spend time catching up, and there was no other option but to walk by moonlight. As we walked, we gave thanks to God, despite Thomas' sore head. We acknowledged that we had been led by Jesus and to see deliverance of a young man who had been bound by anger. We were both blown away.

"He stood like a flippin' statue!" Thomas laughed.

We found some shelter for the night in a disused wooden stable. It wasn't ideal and the smell of the ox and sheep that must have inhabited it once lingered on. Apart from the pong, it was wonderfully warm and Thomas was snoring as soon as he laid down. We were both tired.

Our hope was to rise early, before dawn, but this didn't happen. I woke with a start, the bright rays of the sun shining through the cracks of the wood told me that we had overslept, and not by a short amount of time. The previous day's walk and the encounter with the boys had worn us out and our hope of an extra-long day's walk were dashed by this. Yet we walked as quickly as we could. Sometimes Thomas jogged alongside me, but it was painfully clear to both of us that unless we somehow miraculously met a chariot that had space for two weary travellers, we wouldn't make the Passover evening meal.

Our hope for a miracle didn't come and after a hard day's walk, and with fifteen miles still to go, we decided to look for a place where we could stay. Just before sunset, we had reached the ancient town of Jericho. As we sat in the market square, I breathed out a quick prayer that we would somehow be able to celebrate the Passover, but to be honest it wasn't the symbolism that I wanted. Just food. Any food.

We sat on the edge of the raised wall of a well. The rocks washed smooth by years of water sparkled in the moonlight. It was the fourteenth day of the second month at dusk, and the smell of the cooking lamb braised with bitter herbs and the fresh unleavened bread wafted from the homes surrounding the square made our mouths water. Thomas' stomach protested and instinctively I uttered an 'amen' to his stomach's pained prayer! This made Thomas howl with laughter and a few doors opened ajar to see what the racket was about.

"I see you!" shouted an elderly gent, doubled over silhouetted in the frame of his door with his home filled with light.

"Arh, good evening sir," I replied politely. "Sorry about the noise." And only because we had been taught by Jesus to say it, and for no other reason and without any enthusiasm I ushered "Oh... and peace be with you, by the way."

"Yes, I see you, I see you!" continued the man. "Come, come on in my friends, come and eat with a lonely man, I have cooked way too much to eat by myself and I have enough for two visitors who offer me peace."

Thomas and I looked at each other and lifted our eyes, a sign of relief that we had something to eat, but also to acknowledging the goodness of the Lord in answering our prayers so speedily.

The lintel of his door had already been covered by the blood of the lamb as a reminder of the ancient story from Egypt. Even though I had clearly seen it, as I ducked down to enter his humble home, my hand instinctively reached up to guide me through his small door way. The wet of the fresh blood surprised me and I immediately withdrew my hand to look at it. In the soft light of the man's home I saw blood. I stared at it and all I could think about was Jesus. I was fearful. With my heart racing I wondered how he was, and despite my intense hunger and tiredness I had an urge to run to find him and protect him.

"Please, please, come in and make yourselves at home. As you can see, it is such a simple home, but one where you are most welcome." I snapped out of my panic about Jesus and saw the wooden bowl in the corner full of water, placed in readiness for washing. I cleaned the blood off my hand and rinsed my face ready for the meal. As I did this, the old man spoke about his home, the meal we were about to feast upon and the wine he had saved especially for this occasion.

Every time he said the word 'see' or 'saw' he placed an emphasis on the word and accentuated the 'eee' or 'aaaaw' part of it, and as he did, his frail voice was filled with joy as if he was on the brink of breaking out in giggles.

"I seeeeeee you," he said again. "You two look similar to the two who stayed with me last month. They were kind. They stayed in my home and offered me a greeting of peace, a little like you did in the square."

"You've met followers of Jesus before?" I asked excitedly. He nodded. "That's amazing! Thank you for welcoming us in, sir."

"Yes, I saaaaaaw you out in the square. I seeee you, you seeee!" he said, smiling and holding back laughter.

"I hope you don't find me rude, but why do you keep saying that you 'seeee' us? What do you mean by that? Do you see something in us that made you realise you could welcome us in?" Thomas queried. I was pleased that he had asked the old man, as his phrase was beginning to unnerve me, and even with the beautiful smell of the roasting lamb surrounding me I was wondering whether sitting outside in the cold for another night might be safer than spending a night in a madman's home.

"No, no, no. You don't get it, do you? It's because I seeee you! I seeeeee everything. Crystal clear. I seeeeee!"

We nodded politely, still waiting for an explanation.

"I was born blind." He beamed ear to ear and his eyes sparkled, they were the brightest blue with flecks of grey and green. "Then some Jesus followers healed me and I seeeee. It is the most precious gift that anyone could have ever given me," he laughed. "It's worth more than a vineyard full of gold. Yippee I seeeee!"

We ate our meal with much joy and shared the stories of our adventures, rejoicing in the old man and his transformed life. We spoke together of the wonders we had seen. Thomas' bruised face prompted questions about our day and the meeting of the boys by the river and how the angry young man had been delivered. We also remembered the old story of how the Israelite slaves were instructed to place blood as a mark of protection and a sign that the angel of the Lord would pass over their homes in Egypt. None of us had taken our sandals off, as we would usually have done, and despite the warmth from the fire we kept our cloaks on too, as a reminder of the story of the great Exodus out of Egypt.

It appeared that Passover wasn't the only reason for our new friend's celebration, but each day was lived for the moment. His existence had been loneliness and darkness. He had no family and relied on the mercy of his neighbours to guide him to sit by the side of the road every day. So each day since his sight had been restored he had expected miracles and prayed that people would come for dinner so that he could share his story. Each day it would appear that God would bring at least one person with whom he could share his new-found life.

That night the wine flowed freely. Thomas and I were thirsty and the wine tasted so good, but there were moments when I looked at the red wine in my clay goblet, like the blood on my hand, and I had a fear rise up in my heart. We all ate way too much lamb, leaving none for the morning, as our tradition dictated. Despite the fear within me that sprang up throughout the evening, it was a good night. Thomas reassured me that tomorrow would be even better as we would meet Jesus in Jerusalem and tell him of all that had happened through him granting us his authority to heal the sick. The warmth and the wine caused my head to nod and soon I had drifted off. Our host covered me with a soft woollen blanket.

The streets of Jerusalem were strangely quiet and as we walked through them we heard a roar of a crowd at the far side of the city on a hillside called the 'Place of the skull.' As we approached, Thomas saw some of the disciples watching the ugly scene in the distance. It was a brutal Roman crucifixion, three crosses silhouetted against the charged sky. A thunderstorm was brewing.

"Guys, what the heck are you doing?" Thomas challenged them. Before they could even answer, he derided them and shouted, "Don't stand there and watch such a brutal torture! It's not a sport, you know. Its gross, and you should know better. Now come on, we're looking for Jesus, have you seen him?"

They stood in silence. "Have you not heard Thomas?" someone asked, and then pointed towards the top of the hill where three bodies hung on their crosses.

"They're killing him," one of the followers said coldly. "They arrested him last night and hung him out to die this morning. He's been nailed to that cross for a few hours, now. We can't do anything to help and when we tried to get closer we were threatened by the soldiers."

The sound of the wailing women was getting stronger and stronger as I stood shaking my head.

I wanted to look away but couldn't. From where I stood, I couldn't make out which was the cross Jesus was hanging upon. I walked much closer and as I caught sight of his torn body and battered face I let out a shriek. Doubled over, I vomited. A soldier confronted me and said sternly, "Boy, if you can't handle it, don't watch. Now push off."

"I'm OK, I'm OK," I assured him and stayed rooted to the spot with vomit at my feet and splattered over my beautiful cloak from Sarah.

The clouds were getting thicker and so where the crowds, who were jeering and spitting at the naked men. Most of the abuse was directed towards the middle cross where Jesus hung. His skin had been torn all over his arms and chest. From the open wounds, blood dripped steadily onto the earth, where the crude wood of the cross was supported. My eyes seemed to focus on the blood dripping onto the wet ground beside the soldiers, and for a moment it was as if I had a bird's eye view of the scene. I saw from above the heads of the gambling soldiers squabbling over Jesus' meagre possessions. One of the group of soldiers crouching had blood splattered upon his back and as he stood up I saw that it was him.

Marcus was standing by my Jesus, his face was level with the pierced feet, dripping with blood. I wanted to scream at him, but no sound came out, just a rasping choke. Marcus held a spear in his hand and while his uniform was different from when I had seen him last, it was undoubtedly him.

I watched the scene, unable to move, unable to speak, unable to cry. I watched as the order was given and Marcus pierced the side of Jesus after he had finally given up his last breath and bowed his thorn-crowned head. I watched as blood and clear liquid freely fell from his side. The soldiers lit some crude torches from dried palm branches. The embers darted around. Then a thunderstorm concentrated around the hill and raged. Without any rain. Darkness fell around me. I started to rock back and forth, left to right, as I was physically moved by the ground beneath me shaking. Rocks and small boulders rolled round about me, yet my feet were strangely rooted to the spot. It was then that I heard Marcus shout above the roar of the thunder and earthquake to his fellow soldiers.

"Lads, this bloke must have been the son of God! Look what's happening!" and as he looked around he locked his gaze upon mine and what I saw in that evil bastard's eyes wasn't malice or anger. It was fear. I could kill him. The strong desire for vengeance rose within me, having been buried deep within for years. It burned on my chest, painfully hot as if some of the flying embers had caught my clothes alight. As much as I commanded my legs to walk towards him, they wouldn't and I remained rooted. I closed my eyes and despite the jostling crowds and screams and the moving earth, I could have been alone. I felt utterly alone. Helpless. Then stillness surrounded me, even though the wind blew furiously upon my face, I was cocooned in motionlessness. My ears closed and the shouting howl of the wind around me just became a muffled drone. I strained my ears to try and hear what was happening around me. But the sound went softer and softer, like being underwater, when all the sound from the surface is lost beneath.

"Philip, Philip, Philip..." I heard my name being called but kept my eyes closed. The calling was getting louder and louder but I refused to look.

I sat up. Bolted upright within the simple wooden guest bed, Thomas standing over me, shaking my shoulders and calling my name. "Are you alright Philip?" he asked. "You must have had a nightmare you were making very strange noises. The light from outside shot through the gaps under the door and around the window frame. It was morning.

"They've killed Jesus," I said.

We walked into the city in silence. We arrived in the darkness and storm that I had seen in my vision. They had already taken his body down from the cross and placed him in a borrowed tomb. It wasn't difficult to find John, who we had gotten to know so well during our training. He was one of the closest to Jesus and he had remained long after the crowds had gone. Knelt by the bottom of the hill in the thick dirt. Next to him stood Mary, the mother of Jesus. He was weeping and mumbling "Please Lord, please Lord, save him." But it was too late. Our Rabbi was dead.

Peter was laying low and eventually in the darkness of the night John led us to the place where they had eaten the night before. Towels and a large bowl of water laid discarded on the floor and next to them sat groups of men. Apart from the soft sobbing around the room there was no other sound. Others had joined the twelve and, within the large room, around twenty of us sat. John spoke for the first time, loud and clear.

"Come on, lads!" The shock of his voice in the quiet room brought everyone's gaze upon him. "This can't be it. Can it?" he passionately declared. "We've all seen the miracles and power. The kingdom of heaven can't just stop now, can it?" He looked around but no one was willing to respond. We had all lost hope.

Thomas made up some simple flat bread in the morning, enough for everyone who had stayed overnight. The smell of the bread filled the room, but it didn't stir anyone to investigate breakfast. I had been awake for many hours but hadn't moved, just watched Thomas scurry about making the dough and baking it on the simple fireplace.

Had it just been down to me, I would have chosen to do nothing for the rest of the day. Just sit. The shock had paralysed me and the only thing I had thought that I could physically do was make my way back to Sarah. I longed for her embrace. I longed for someone who could listen to how I felt. Who knew me. Life was now crap. We had put our all into following Jesus and now he was gone. Dead. My life had been turned upside down by him. Now the one who had healed me through my mum, given me a purpose and a hope in life, was no more.

Thomas asked me to go and buy some fruit and when I didn't respond he pulled me up from the wooden floor and placed some coins in my hand. Firmly.

"Go," he commanded.

I walked out into the city in a daze. The sun felt strange upon my face. The warmth felt out of place and so did the people rushing around me, laughing, talking, and going about their daily business. It was as if nothing had happened and the death of Jesus was just a bit of entertainment for the Passover celebrations. Over breakfast we gradually spoke, in soft tones, about what had happened, pausing when it became too much to speak of. We heard how Jesus had been arrested and Thomas and I learnt that it had been Judas who had betrayed him. Had tried to force Jesus' hand in becoming king.

Judas had believed that the kingdom that Jesus spoke of was the literal overthrow of Rome and its occupation of Israel. He believed that Jesus would cause an uprising that would give freedom to our land once more. When he saw that the plan of the Pharisees was to execute Jesus under the charge of blasphemy, Judas regretted what he had done and in desperation pleaded with the chief priests to release him. When his wish wasn't granted, he had killed himself.

I knew how he felt. Until the following morning, that is. I wished that Judas had been able to wait three days – because, on the first day of the week after Jesus had died, the greatest miracle of all happened. First the women and then Peter and John reported that they had seen him and that he risen from the dead!

Soon, many more of the followers shared their encounters of seeing Jesus in different places. On the road while travelling, by the beach, in locked rooms when people ate together. It was what each one of us longed for: to see him alive, risen from the dead. I too longed to catch a glimpse of him and believe with my eyes as well as my heart what had happened.

Confidence grew amongst the followers, and those who had left Jerusalem and had given up hope returned, inspired once more that they could change the world for Jesus. He had done the impossible, risen from the grave and defeated the curse of death over humankind. He was victorious and the realisation that Jesus was alive though he had been dead dawned upon us. Someone summed it perfectly as we excitedly spoke together one evening: "You know what this means? It proves that Jesus really is who he says he is. This verifies that this is 100% real!"

8. My Journey

Early one morning I made my way to get to the market stalls first and choose the best pickings for our breakfast. The growing number of followers meant that it wasn't possible to eat together, but we moved around the dozen or so shared houses across the city to eat, pray and introduce more people to the idea that Jesus is the messiah. Our shared life was attractive, and those who had shared with those who lacked. Despite the smaller groups across the city we were able to meet publicly in the temple courts, and this is where many more people encountered healing and heard what we believed about Jesus.

There were always stacks of fresh fish in the market but it was the fruit that I was tasked to provide for our meals. Plenty of grapes, a basket or two of pomegranates if they were good, and on this occasion I was asked to fetch some sweet dried dates. Being a regular, I nodded to the market stall seller who greeted me with a smile. I asked if I could try one of the grapes before I committed to buying the whole lot.

"You must have had a few bunches for free by now, one by one!" he teased. The juice filled my mouth with summery sweetness, they were good. I closed my eyes to savour the taste and it was at that very moment I heard the voice. It was gentle, but like large waves smashing against rocks time and time again. He stood behind me.

"I think your cloak is wonderful! I especially love the fish symbol." Turning towards the voice, the weight of his beautiful presence made me bow low and I went to grab and hold on to his feet but he quickly grabbed my wrists and lifted me up.

His strong arms brought me eye to eye. "It's all right Philip. Come on, let's walk and talk." He spoke first as we walked away from the market stall. "What I told Sarah is all true. I am calling you to fish for people. You will be an evangelist."

I turned to look at him once more, face to face, and I saw in his kind eyes that he had faith in me, that this wasn't wishful thinking. I closed my eyes and shook my head.

"Please, Jesus. Me? I mean, look at me! How can I fish for people?" I held my empty hands towards him and cried, "I have nothing."

"I know," he smiled, "That's why I'm calling you."

9

My Seven Years

AD 29, 15 years old

Each day there was a new buzz in the city. We were growing and flourishing and many more Jesus-like miracles broke out across the city – some of them so dramatically life-changing that the Apostles often got in trouble with the authorities, some even to the point of being put in prison or flogged. Despite this, people travelled from all over the region to ask for prayer and learn about the Messiah. Each night you could freely choose from a number of synagogues or homes to go and listen to the teachings of Jesus and encounter the signs of his kingdom.

The healing miracles blew me away and, having seen my own foot completely restored and the life-changing difference it had made, I always rejoiced and danced with those who had encountered healing similar to mine. Despite my self-doubt and times of loneliness, we really did live in exciting times. We were making history. The weight of God's presence through his Spirit brooded over the city and, while I couldn't quite get my head around how Jesus could perform multiple miracles all over the place, it was so good to be an eye witness to his new kingdom advancing on earth as it is in heaven.

It's hard to convey the enormousness of this, but having known Jesus as a walking, talking man in the flesh, seeing now that with one mention of his name people where fully made whole, well, this just blew me away! It's as if each one of us was becoming like small Christs and it's this label that others had started to use unkindly as a means to taunt. The word 'Christians' began to stick and soon it described what our community of disciples were all about. We were becoming like Christ, yet I also carried a deep doubt that Jesus had really called me.

It didn't take long until I carried my secret like a valuable necklace hidden under my clothes. Precious, out of sight but near to my heart. I felt it every day. Closely. I wasn't the only one who had a story to share of meeting with Jesus after he had come back to life. Only mine remained untold. The followers gathered together in one of the jam-packed homes across the city in the early evenings, with the flames flickering and catching the sparkling eyes excitedly retelling one story that followed another until the early morning hours and soon a river of stories of encountering the risen Jesus filled the city. But mine never got to join that flow.

All the stories I heard were magical, the kinds of stories that make you laugh and cry at the same time. I just couldn't find the words to retell mine. It felt like the depth of the short conversation I had with Jesus was like years of talking normally. How could I share it? It's not like I wouldn't have found empathy amongst my fellow disciples, and knowing this nearly made me speak out. On a few occasions I had literally opened my mouth to speak in one of the rare lulls around the warm fire, but the words remained stuck in my throat. You see, I felt like the call from him was too big while I simply felt too little. How would anyone believe that I was called to announce the good news?

It was in those early years of belonging to the disciples in Jerusalem that I managed to convince myself that no-one would actually believe me if I told them that I was called by Jesus to fish for people. Besides, I hadn't heard of anyone being called an 'evangelist' before, and to announce that I was one felt way too presumptuous. And ambitious. I mean, give me a simple job to do and I was a happy chappy, but to go and fish for people? Not me, surely?

Yet I couldn't forget that market encounter with Jesus, and for many years whenever I recalled it and no-one was around to see, I would buy some grapes and talk to Jesus about it while eating them. The blissful remembering felt way too perfect while I felt way too dirty. And too small. Jesus and I had continued to walk on that day out of the market to talk. Like friends. He spoke with me about my future and how I was going to be sent to proclaim the good news of him. And, as he spoke, he placed his rough, scarred hand upon my chest. The very place where my secret now hung like a pendant. In hushed tones, he told me that all people needed to know that they were loved beyond their wildest dreams. It was at that moment that my heart burned with a deep longing for people to encounter the weight of his love for them. Just as I had felt and known without a doubt that I was loved.

Jesus explained to me that he had freely laid down his life. Even in the midst of the arrest and betrayal he had had the choice of whether to die as a sacrifice for the world. Or not. He chose to give his life up and was happy that he had.

"You see, Philip," he explained, "God loved the world so much he gave me to die for you, and then to live again to show that I truly am the Messiah." It was then that he paused and looked at me, breathed in

163

deeply and then, laughing, exhaled and said these words:

"I am the lamb who takes away the sin of the world." I felt his breath upon my face and as he said those words I sensed the power of the perfect sacrifice taking away my sin. It was as if I had started over again. Made new.

Like praying with grapes, in rare times of hiding away from the business of the growing community I would climb one of the seven hills around the city and face the warm breeze at the hill's brow. It was then that I would close my eyes and imagine Jesus standing before me uttering those words. They became a daily prayer for me when I would walk from one house to another and I would breathe in: 'Look, the lamb of God…" and then breathe out, "…who takes away the sin of the world.'

I didn't see Jesus again after that day in the market, but the first friends of Jesus saw him ascend to heaven. I had missed it. Because of this and, I guess, my own self-doubt, I started to believe that the commission Jesus had given me to go and announce his news to all people must have been a mistake. That somehow he had chosen the wrong Philip. Crazy, I know. So, instead of responding to his call to go alongside the other disciples, I stayed and continued to serve and help with fetching provisions and preparing food. And thoughts of leaving the city to be an evangelist were soon gone.

It was when Jesus and the closest group of disciples were on the hillside that he had told them to wait as he was going to send the promise of power. It was the Spirit that would enable us to be witnesses in Jerusalem, Judea, and Samaria and then to the ends of the world. This power did come, dramatically, some weeks later – and on the very first day 3,000 people were added to the growing community. Yet, alongside all the others I remained in Jerusalem and we all soon kind of forgot that the Spirit was given for the ends of the earth.

Despite my lack of confidence in going as an evangelist, though, there remained an itch for adventure, a longing to see more and more people come to know the living Messiah. But the opportunity for the kind of exploits Thomas and I had gone on before never happened, and I guess I was immersed in the new growing church. I was also on hand to explain and pray for those who joined our community, and while this satisfied the itch to an extent, I never dared step forward for preaching or the training sessions that we held in homes across the city. So my call remained hidden.

I faithfully kept on serving for seven years and, while I had the privilege of seeing the disciples grow dramatically in number, no-one knew about my meeting with Jesus in the market place that late warm afternoon.

The growing church was busy and there was always something to do. I was needed, and this felt good. And the busyness of doing practical work counteracted my self-doubt as to whether I was called by Jesus or not. Over the years in Jerusalem I concluded that it really must have been wishful thinking on my part or perhaps he had made a mistake.

Despite the exhilaration of the wonders and the transformation we saw in people's lives, the first friends of Jesus (who people referred to as the Apostles) were overworked and increasingly getting tired. Not only did they teach in the temple courts on most days, pray for the sick and counsel those who were coming to a new faith, they also looked after the distribution of food for the widows and the neediest in our community.

Some of our new followers took it upon themselves to watch every day who got what provisions and, instead of helping the apostles, they carried on spying at the distribution points and complained to them instead! On most days these people, who seemed to have nothing better to do, arranged to meet with the already stretched apostles to moan. This, in my opinion, took way too much of their valuable time. I often saw them locked in some lengthy discussion about it and I became concerned that this small part of the work of the growing church would distract from the other areas that we were called to do. Yet those who complained felt ever so strongly about the issue and they kept voicing that 'too many outsiders took too much bread!' One or two of the needy were accused of selling the bread in the market place and spending the money on wine.

While the complainers may have had a point, I didn't agree with their ideas about who should be allowed food or not. The distribution was a symbol of shared grace, of the life of Jesus freely given to all. Yet, from what I could see, the distribution had become a bit hit and miss and if a widow neglected to turn up at the designated place at the right time she simply went without. So, the frailest in our community were being neglected and even if they did manage to get to the distribution house before the others, often the healthier stronger ones pushed their way to the front to grab what they could carry. What was meant to be for good was turning bad. From what I could see, it could be remedied through a bit of organisation. It was around this time when I shared with James, one of the apostles, about a proposal for the distribution of the bread, that the church decided that Deacons would be appointed to be in charge.

I was chosen, along with six other men. Out of the thousands of other followers of Jesus that lived in and around the city, I was chosen amongst the seven. When I heard the news I felt like a fraud. The first thought that sprang to mind was 'if only they knew my doubts.'

It's kind of funny, but when the Deacons were chosen, all I could think about was one of the first stories I remember my dad telling me about King David. Being born lame, I connected with the insignificance of how King David must have felt when he was anointed. He was the smallest and youngest brother amongst his larger, stronger siblings. I must have been four or five when he told me that story. We were sitting in our yard. Mum was ill and had gone to bed and dad picked me up in his strong arms and placed me on his knee. He had the largest, strongest hands, with nicks and cuts all over that I liked to feel and ask questions about, and on his left hand his thumb nail was a strange shade of bluey green. I remember holding his thumbs with my hands while he retold how David was looking after the sheep when Samuel had turned up to anoint the new king.

You see, it wasn't just the insignificance of David that resonated with me. It was the fact that when my name was announced to serve as a Deacon, I, like David, was nowhere to be found. In the story, he's looking after the family's sheep, miles away from the hubbub and excitement of the prophet coming to town to choose a new king amongst all the sons of Jesse.

When my name was called in the church meeting I was daydreaming by the river about Sarah. I didn't learn about my new appointment until the meeting was over and the others had been prayed for. Instead of boosting my confidence in what Jesus had called me to do, in a strange way becoming a Deacon reinforced the sense I carried every day of being torn. I was torn by the fact that Jesus had called me to something great but I simply didn't feel up to the task. I also felt torn about Sarah. I thought of her every day and yearned to be with her. Of course, I was loyal to the community of believers that I served, but longed for my love.

Becoming a Deacon somehow sealed the fate that I would never marry. Sarah couldn't wait for me and I knew that. Besides, her aunt would surely have found another husband for her from Samaria. While there was a sense of authority about the new role of Deacon, taking it carried with a deep sense of aloneness, and in the business of serving and helping I felt isolated.

I'm ashamed to admit it, but one evening I was drawn to the area in Jerusalem where the prostitutes sold sex for a few denarii. I longed to be held and loved. I sat on the side of the road with the house I intended to enter in sight. I needed the coast to be clear, and as I waited with money in my belt and ready to pull my cloak over my head and go into the building, I heard Jesus speak. 'Heard' isn't the right way to describe what happened. It had been a few years since we had spoken together in the market and this time when I heard his voice again, it was deeply within me yet unmistakably Jesus. Like a thousand scrolls being spoken into me. Yet there were only eight words that I heard in a split second. This is what I felt Jesus say to me: 'I have called you because you love me.'

I walked home knowing my purpose and call afresh and even though being faithful to Jesus meant I wouldn't see Sarah again, I knew that it was worth the cost. Painful though it was.

It was one of the busiest days that I was on duty for the distribution of the food with another Deacon called Stephen, a man who had very quickly became a good friend of mine. It was the busiest afternoon of the week as the following day, being the Sabbath, we didn't give out any food and double portions where distributed instead. What we did on the holy day was spend much of our time together, singing new songs of praise and hearing one of the first friends of Jesus share some of the teachings of how we could grow as followers. All of this was interspersed with good food, wine and laughter. It was a treat to relax on the Sabbath after a busy week serving and it was on this particular day that I was grateful for Stephen's help.

He was much taller than me and was able to lift entire baskets of bread like I could lift a single loaf. He always wore dark brown and coupled with his height this made him stand out from the rest of us. Deacons were chosen for the qualities of being filled with the Holy Spirit and faith, and while I could clearly see this in Stephen I struggled to know how they could have seen this it me. But I was chosen and, even though I carried self-doubt like a familiar cloak, I was still able to step up into the role of serving – and my plans for a better distribution of provisions were already working after a month.

We had heard of a famine south of the Dead Sea. The reputation of the church in Jerusalem brought some desperate visitors in need of help and that day, unbeknown to us, we would see the greatest number arrive in one day.

They all wore black and their robes dragged upon the dusty ground. The group of seven approached us and one of them asked in a quiet, husky voice, "We're looking for where the followers of Jesus distribute food. We haven't eaten for days and we are very hungry. Can you tell us where to find them?"

Stephen reassured them they had come to the right place and that there was a little food that we could share with them. We also had a little wine and fresh water that they could drink. Five of them sat on the ground by the small square yard of our simple home which acted as the food distribution point. Two didn't sit but rather went back the way they had travelled, quickly. Thinking this somewhat strange I asked why they had left in such a hurry.

"To fetch the others. They'll be back soon..." one replied.

We barely had enough food for the small handful that had caught us at the end of our distribution, let alone for any more people. Stephen grabbed my arm and pulled me to one side.

"Philip, I will go and fetch some more food from the market, I have a few coins and I will gather as much as I can. These poor people must be starving. They really must have something to eat today. I will pray as I go."

I was grateful for his prayers as minutes later a large group of thirty to forty women and children turned the corner and waved at the small group already seated by the house. A similar sized group followed close behind them, which included frail older members. Some looked very ill and were being carried on crude wooden stretchers that looked as if they would fall apart any moment. The dirty, torn cloth that held them together had given up at some of the corners and the patients sagged beneath where they were being carried.

I stood at the doorway and greeted as many as I could with a blessing of peace. Yes, sharing the peace of the Lord was an important aspect of what we did, but it was also partly to stall for time until Stephen came back, and to hide behind me what meagre provisions we had in store. I closed the door behind me and handed out the water in clay cups, which they shared amongst themselves.

One of the travellers said that they had been mugged on the way and lifted up his sleeve to show cuts and bruises along his right arm. Another man had been badly beaten about the head – when the thieves couldn't find anything of value in their group they had picked on him in a rage and would have killed him if it hadn't been for the rest, who tore off the attackers. They sat quietly in small groups. The children sat and stared at me. They were silent. This was unnerving. It was as' if they had given up crying. This group was new to the city and desperate.

I hurried around, greeting the large group and, with each one I met, at the back of my mind I thought of the sparse provisions we had to give them. I had

173

two loaves, some cooked white fish in a small bowl and a bunch of sweet eating-grapes. It was food for two and Stephen and I were planning to eat it together later, once we had cleared up. But I knew we needed to give our food to the weakest of the new guests.

I waited for an hour for Stephen but he didn't come back. I busied myself attending to those who had arrived and laying hands on some for healing. Eventually the leader of the group stood up and held my hand.

"Please, good sir, may we have some food now? We are so hungry. We have no way to pay for it other than our thanks and whatever work we can we will gladly do. But please, have mercy on us." He looked longingly at the closed wooden door of the small house.

I nodded and also looked over at the door where he was gazing and then looked down at my feet. "The thing is..." I said quietly so that the others wouldn't hear, "We only have a small amount left. It's late in the day and we have given all we had to the widows and orphans in our community already. But my friend will be back soon with more."

But Stephen didn't come back.

After another ten minutes I walked over to the door and a few of the group followed closely behind, peering over my shoulder as we walked. I went to open the door with my outreached hand pushing the door as usual and carried a dread in the pit of my stomach while I stood ready for it to swing open I felt as if I had offered false hope and many of the group would be painfully disappointed with me. They had heard of the goodness of the followers of Jesus in Jerusalem and our reputation that had spread over fifty miles away was just about to be dashed to pieces.

The door didn't budge. Something was jamming it from the inside which confused me as all we had was a table on the far side of the wall and some empty baskets. I leant into the door and pushed with all my might, and it moved gradually, making a scraping, dragging sound as it moved heavily inwards. At first I thought it may be Stephen playing some kind of practical joke, and I called out, "That's not funny you know!"

But there was no answer. Inside were brand new woven baskets covered with pure white cloth that concealed their contents. They were stacked upon the table. In each of the corners of the room stood clay water urns with yellow painted lids made from crafted wood with a layer of cork. The object that had hindered me opening the door was a large earthen bowl full of cooked fish with lemon and herbs upon the top. The smell wafted out and, as each of the weary travellers caught a scent of fresh bread and fish, a satisfying thankful groan spread about where they were sat. What had been prepared for us wasn't just food to distribute. It was a banquet. There was more than enough.

As they ate, laughter filled the street. Children started chatting and shrieking with joy, which attracted more people to come to join us. Some of those who begged but never wanted help from us sat on the edges of the group and enjoyed the food. Soon some of the men from the church heard of the miracle and came to see for themselves.

"Well done, Philip!" one of the apostles cheered as they slapped me on the back. "Great job!"

"I am as shocked as you are. I really didn't do a thing. This is all the Lord's doing!" I said.

What struck me about that miracle was the amount. It was lavish. It was over the top. There was wine in two of the vessels. It was the best I had ever tasted. In the other two were honey and in the other the most luxurious dried fruit, some of which we simply didn't recognise. But it tasted so good. The crowd lingered and James, whom I had spoken to about the distribution those weeks back and had run from the other side of the city to see what had happened, retold my story. The crowd were now satisfied and full.

He made me stand next to him and said, "The food we have feasted upon today wasn't here when you arrived. Seriously, get this, everyone. This man..." he put his arms around me and continued, "He had enough food for only two people when you arrived. Behind this closed door," he pointed to the wooden door of the store room behind us, "...the Lord Jesus himself performed a miracle. This is a sign of his great love for you. He knows each one of you. You have been led here, it's not an accident. You are here not just for a meal but to feast upon the news that the one who can do these kinds of miracles says that he is the 'bread of life'!"

James continued in his familiar demonstrative fashion and after ten minutes or so I slipped away from him and joined the crowds as he gesticulated with his arms and moved around in front of them, zig-zagging one way then the other, excited as to what the Lord had done. While the fish had been eaten up, there was plenty of bread and dried fruits for the following day.

Around half of those who had gathered for a meal wanted to welcome Jesus as their Lord, and we made plans to mark their new commitments with baptisms sometime in the week – until one of the new guests, dressed in a torn black cloak shouted, "Why not now?!"

I led the group down to the river and in the sunset over fifty people were baptised. James and I did most of the baptising, although it was James who spoke publicly and led people in their declaration of new faith in Jesus the Christ.

Stephen never did show up.

Later on, I got to learn that while on his own in the market buying what he could for the refugees he had been arrested. It was while I patiently waited with the large group of hungry travellers that he had already been thrown into prison. He was also badly beaten.

The joy of baptising the new believers and the celebration we all revelled in at the miracle of the provision of food soon died. It was as if such a mighty furthering of the kingdom brought a vicious evil attack. Soon after that glorious feast Stephen was killed.

I watched it all from a distance as he was hauled out from the temple where he had been faced trial and rocks were flung into him with such force and hatred. Despite some thudding at his head as they landed, his face still shone. He radiated like a young man in love. His cheeks looked out of place as he knelt in the dirt with his own blood dripping down upon it. He loved Jesus through and through and this showed until his very last breath.

The mind-blowing miracles were faith-affirming but losing Stephen came like a flood over the excitement of being a Christian and my Deacon role with the church. To be candid, it made me lose hope. He was the strongest one of us and without his support I didn't know if I could continue. But it was much more than that. He had been my friend. Not only had I lost my first proper friend in Sarah, I had now lost him. He had always had a cheeky word that made me laugh – like the time I refused to give four loaves of bread to Martha, one of the widows. She had lost her husband nearly twenty years ago but had never wanted to remarry. Once Stephen whispered to me jokingly, with Martha standing in front of us, that it was really because she was so large and no one would want to marry her anyway in fear of being crushed! (Thankfully this was out of earshot.)

On that occasion, though, I only allowed Martha to have three loaves instead of her usual four. Stephen stood next to the elderly widow, towering above both of us and pointing at me he said in a serious accusing voice, "What are you insinuating, Philip? That Martha needs to go on a diet?!"

I wasn't the only one to lose heart. It was my idea to postpone the distribution of food for a while, even though some of the other Deacons wanted to continue to distribute provisions. But now, under cover of darkness, I laid low. We all feared that our lives could be lost in the same way that Stephen's had been.

179

It was around this time that some of the community left the city to re-join their families in other parts of Israel. The rest of us stayed and took stock. We decided that the best use of time was to stay hidden in our homes and simply to pray. To be honest, it felt like a cop-out. But we were frightened. I stayed in a house with some of the apostles. It was hard to imagine that the favour we had experienced in Jerusalem for nearly seven years was changing fast. There was talk of the man who had been responsible for the killing of Stephen being on a mission to wipe out the church.

Saul was a well-respected Pharisee who had convinced the rulers of the temple that the church was a blasphemy against God. It was some months later, after laying low, when I would see Saul face to face. It felt like the worst of the trouble had passed, and I went alongside a dozen others to hear my original mission partner Thomas preach once more at the Synagogue of the Isles. It was there that I encountered Saul's hatred face to face.

The gathering was packed. The synagogue had easily been the busiest around Jerusalem and tonight people peered through the open windows and stood along the wall inside at least four rows deep, and all the available seats on the floor where taken up. There was an expectancy about the meeting. For many like me it had been a long time since we had met together openly. But it felt safe to us and besides, the Synagogue felt like an official and familiar place to meet. We weren't hiding. What we had was open for all to see.

Some people had brought family and friends who needed healing and already there had been testimony of people encountering the Lord Jesus through the prayers and ministry we offered, even before the meeting started. One man said that even before he even sat down his eyes had been opened! Thomas was a good man and carried a measure of grace that others like me simply didn't. He epitomised the saying of Jesus that 'It is not the healthy who need a doctor, but the sick.' Thomas wore this truth wherever he went. He had been forgiven so much by Jesus that when he encountered people who believed they were beyond the pale of being forgiven he would share his story of how he had met with Jesus. People always sat up and listened to what he had to say once they knew something of his background, and tonight was no different. He stood at the front and indicated with his arms for the hubbub to die down. His opening prayer brought about the most beautiful presence of the Lord. The Spirit fell upon us and intertwined with Thomas' prayer like a poem, dancing and skipping upon us. Some broke out laughing, which caused others to give disapproving looks and tut-tut noises echoed around the room.

"It's all right, sisters and brothers," Thomas reassured. "The Spirit is with us and it is in his presence with us that we encounter fullness of joy. He brings about joy where there hasn't been any."

Thomas spoke eloquently. It lasted over an hour, but felt more like a few minutes. I longed for such a gift and, as I was thinking about what it would be like to have a gift like his, he spoke about Jesus coming back to life after being crucified. It was then that there was a scream from the far-left corner of the building. It was fairly dark in the room, so no one knew who had screamed the word 'blasphemy!' but there, at the back of the crowded room, stood Saul.

He was shorter than I had remembered from when Stephen had been murdered. He wore a black cloak with a bright red trim that made him look almost like a Roman soldier. He had worn this cloak over his head and hidden amongst the crowds sitting on the floor, unrecognisable to those around him. As he stood, he pulled his cloak from his head and strode forward. His mouth was contorting but no sounds were coming out of it. The light caught the spit sputtering as he mouthed angry words and curses.

Thomas stopped mid-sentence and froze as Saul, who was now accompanied by two guards, strode over the crowds to the front, without any care of who they trod on or kicked in their hurry to get to where Thomas stood. Those sitting on the floor peeled back, making a pathway before him, but some were still hurt by the carelessness of the guards. A toddler screamed as his fingers were crushed under the heavy boot of one of them. A young woman was pulled aside by her hair by the other as he strode closer and closer. Her screams went ignored. Some people turned to look for a place to run, but whispers about the entrance being blocked by even more guards with swords rippled out through the jam-packed room.

Saul also brandished a sword and, while his was smaller than those of the temple guards, he was waving it in front of him as he made his way towards Thomas. Half way across the room an older man called Joseph whom I had helped baptise a few months previously stood up:

"Now stop right there, young man!" he shouted but, without breaking stride, Saul's sword whipped him across his face and the sound of the flat of the metal blade breaking Joseph's cheek bone caused a gasp amongst everyone assembled. Other than the steady thud of Saul and the thug's feet on the synagogue floor, the whole space was silent. Then the stillness was broken by the shriek of a young child who cried out in fear for their mummy, who reassured them with a calming, gentle hush.

Joseph had gone flying by the force of Saul's blade and he was knocked out cold. He lay unconscious and somewhat awkwardly sprawled on the floor, one leg bent unpleasantly while the other remained straight towards the back of the synagogue, almost pointing towards the door. He was bleeding profusely from his face. Those around him attended to him as much as they could. I saw that he was still breathing, and with the flow of blood now stemmed I was sure that he would be alright.

Saul reached Thomas.

Thomas stood with his arms wide but low to his side in a peaceful manner. Without any concern and with a surprising element of warmth in his voice he stated,

"Brother Saul. You are most welcome to talk with me, but we can't allow that kind of behaviour in this place of worship. Now please, let's sit down and we can talk together."

"Worship?!" screamed Saul. "How dare you speak of worship!" he hissed. "I worship the living God. You... you worship some dead Nazarene scum. He does not live. Your simple carpenter was nothing but an uneducated trickster. Your Jesus is not alive. He's rotting in the ground dead, where you will be rotting sent to hell for your blasphemy Thomas. We all know who you are, you filthy, filthy, disgusting, prostitute."

Saul's rage made him spit and Thomas calmly wiped the saliva off his face before saying,

"Jesus loves you Saul. He laid down his life for you and to prove he was the son of God, he then..."

Without a word Saul struck wildly out with his sword, aiming right at Thomas' face. Thomas impulsively held up his right arm and the blade of the sword cut deeply into his wrist and for a split moment it remained stuck deep in his arm. It was then that I ran forward to help. It was pure instinct. As I ran to the front, I shouted firmly: "No, in Jesus name."

Saul jerked his sword out of the side of Thomas' arm and turned it towards me, ready to lunge, but instead he simply stood fixed to the spot, with his arm aloft with Thomas' blood dripping onto his forehead and trickling down his face. The blade was covered red.

"Arrest these bastards," he ordered the guards and turned towards the exit. "The rest of you. If you are caught meeting under the pathetic name of Jesus once more you will all be thrown in prison."

The crowd was silent.

As he strode towards the door, he suddenly stopped. He lingered by Joseph, who had now come round and was gazing up at Saul, laying at his feet mouthing some silent prayers which I couldn't hear. The right side of his face was bruised and swollen and right in the middle of it there was a deep, broad gash from the top of his right ear to the side of his mouth. Without looking down, Saul clenched his sword in his fist and with one downward action he thrust it firmly by into Joseph's neck as he lay by his feet.

I slipped in his blood as I was manhandled out the door with Thomas. The warmth of it soaked the side of my outer garment and through onto my leg, but in that moment my concern wasn't for the precious gift from Sarah. It meant nothing as I looked at the man whom I had baptised, the man I had had the joy of seeing saved by Jesus, now dead. Motionless on the floor.

Outside of the Synagogue Saul had amassed even more soldiers. Thomas and I were held roughly, our wrists forced behind our backs. We faced Saul, who grabbed at the closest woman and tore off her shawl to clean his sword. The snatching spun her around and she landed on her behind, which made the soldiers laugh and point at the woman sat, undignified, on the ground. Saul threw the bloodied garment onto her and screamed: "Anyone else want a taste of my sword tonight? You blaspheming shits! You had better not meet here ever again."

By now people were streaming out of the synagogue, running as fast as their legs would carry them, some with children in their arms, while the guards jeered and spat at them. It was a game to them. As we watched the last of the people running out from the building, Thomas and I were tied to a wooden cart ready to be taken to prison where we knew we would face beatings, if we were fortunate. Most likely it would be death, going by what we had seen with our friend Stephen and now Joseph.

Thomas stood next to me and I looked at him, ready for some reassurance from my strong friend. At first I thought he was praying. But all he mouthed over and over was 'Oh shit.' I carried on staring at Thomas until Saul turned to look at us and screamed, "Where the hell is he?"

Unsure as to who he meant, I looked around, scanning the scene. I was certain that it was just me and Thomas who had been tied up and arrested and wondered who else was going to join us in prison. But then he launched at Thomas, grabbing his chin and cheeks in his hands, squeezing so tightly that the white of Thomas' teeth showed through Saul's grip.

"Where has he gone?" Saul screamed, spitting once more in his face. Thomas turned his neck, still with Saul's hand grasping his face, fingers digging deep into his cheeks. He looked right into my face and through a muffled mouth he said, "He was just here, I swear. I don't know where he's gone." I looked at Thomas blankly and was just about to speak when Saul leant forward and lifted his knee. I saw what he was going to do. He landed the weight of his body in between Thomas' legs and pulled back. Thomas pulled upon the rope crudely tied to his wrists and tried to double up with the pain but the ropes prevented him from doing so. He let out a loud cry.

When they tore the ropes off his wrists what was revealed looked to be two dark bracelets, red blistered trinkets dripping with red beads. They dragged him away, leaving me standing in the flickering light of the torches. I wasn't in the shadows – having stood right next to Thomas, we were both visible in the torchlight. No one seemed to see me. Even when one of the guards lingered behind while the others trotted off with Thomas, he hurriedly urinated right by where I stood by the cart, narrowly missing me. He simply didn't see me. Yet I was right there.

It was in the faint morning light that I awoke with a start. The entrance to the synagogue was open and inside the torch light flickered, revealing the ruler of the synagogue clearing up the mess, mostly made by Joseph's blood. My head pounded and I ached all over from where I had stood tied to the cart for hours. I then observed members of Joseph's family carrying his body away and the synagogue leader standing from scrubbing the floor, crying with the family. Even though he had done a good job washing the blood away, once the family had left I saw him once more through the open door return to his hands and knees scrubbing at the brown tiles. And though the place was a hive of activity no one noticed me by the old cart.

It wasn't until the sun had fully risen and the nearby cockerels' competing cries were well underway, trying to outdo each other, that I saw the woman. The one I had seen the night before, the one whose scarf had been used by Saul, had come back looking for it. It lay trampled and filthy.

"Excuse me," I said gently. "Is there any way you could help me?" I looked upwards for eye contact and this caused my shoulders and back to cry out in pain.

"Why did they leave you here?" She asked as she untied my wrists.

"I really don't know," I humbly replied as I shook out my arms in front of me. I leaned backwards and forwards to try and free the knotted muscles in my lower back.

"Can I fetch you anything?" Her kindness made me think that I really should linger and eat something but then thoughts from the attack and Saul's threats caused adrenaline to rush into my body and I knew I needed to take flight.

I ran with all my might along the very path that had brought me to Jerusalem with Thomas seven years previously. It was only after around five miles that I stopped to walk, still looking back every few minutes to make sure I wasn't being followed. When I had found a sheltered spot I washed in the river and tried to get the ugly stains that blotted all along my left side from my garments. Mementos from where I had slipped in the blood. The dried brown blood turned a peculiar red in the river water and, as I pounded and scrubbed my clothes, I remembered that painful day when I had found my Sarah.

I felt more alone than I had ever felt before. I was frightened and, as I dressed in my damp, stained clothes, I knew there was only one place I could run to.

10

Our Meeting

AD 36, 22 years old

He had changed. He looked mellower and appeared to have grown taller, but that may have been more to do with how he held his head. He looked different. Unashamed. Full of peace. I kept these thoughts to myself but he announced, as if he had a large audience, how different I looked and he said over and over, shaking his head,

"The boy has become a man!"

He continued to pour his encouragements deeply into me and even before he offered me something to eat or drink or had asked me why I had called at his home after so many years, he took me by my hands and looked me in the eyes and spoke those words that seemed to keep me going.

"Everything is going to be alright, Philip. You know that, don't you?'

I hadn't been given the opportunity to let him know what I had been through over the past week, so the significance of those familiar words caused me to sink deeply into his arms and he gave me a bear hug. I wanted to believe his words, but I felt too young to have witnessed the cruel death of my close friend, and then Joseph the old man whom Saul had murdered in front of us. I began to shake as he held me, as the shock began to sink in.

My sobbing didn't faze him and as he held me it felt like he had been guessing when I would arrive; it felt like he had stood waiting with his big arms wide open for my return, ready to find an embrace where I could release all the aching and anguish I felt. This was a God moment.

Eventually, after a meal, I explained to Shimon that I needed a safe haven from the horrors that I had witnessed in Jerusalem. To illustrate this, I stood and indicated the stain on the right hand side of the cloak that I had tried to wash. Shimon looked at it for what seemed like an age. As he did, it was his turn to break. His tears fell down his cheeks and, as they fell, he spoke in a warble within the sobs.

"But Jesus brings joy and peace. He brings new life and meaning. How could they kill people for following him? It's not as if he's some kind of terrorist! What do they fear?"

I tried to answer his questions but found it difficult to talk. He gently explained that I could stay for as long as I needed, but there was less room in his home now that his wife Elizabeth and their three young children filled it.

When they returned from the market, our sadness from my news about the church in Jerusalem was interrupted by laughter. Lots of it. Games of chase, farms and races sparked off around us as Shimon and I sat together on the smooth courtyard floor, soaking in the scenes the children created around us. Seeing them full of joy brought a sense of healing and safety for that moment, and I knew I had made the right decision to venture back to Beth Shean.

We continued to talk late into the night, and when the children were fast asleep, slouched on their parents' laps, Elizabeth joined our conversation.

"Shimon has told me a great deal about you and your friend Thomas."

I held back the sadness thinking of him while Elizabeth continued to speak of all that the Lord had been doing since we were with them last and how, over the seven years since the time that I had stayed with Shimon, thirty more from the city had been dramatically healed and where living by the teachings of Jesus. They were serving as accidental leaders of the emerging church in their town.

"We owe so much to you, Philip," Elizabeth went on. "Without your obedience to come here to share the good news those years ago, we wouldn't be the people we are today. We wouldn't even have each other!" And with that, she gave Shimon a sloppy kiss on his cheek and they both giggled like one of their own children now asleep on their laps, exhausted from their carefree exuberant play.

It was at the moment of that playful kiss that once more I thought of Sarah. There was a heaviness in my heart due to being full of regret for not coming sooner to look for her. I knew deep down that I had missed my chance of being with her. Sitting with Shimon and Elizabeth, looking at them, I acknowledged that it would have been unreasonable for me expect her to wait for me. Seven years had gone too quickly for me in Jerusalem, as if I had lived in some kind of different time zone to the rest of the world.

It was the buzz and excitement that penetrated every day, of seeing lives changed and people physically healed, even of skin diseases that had disappeared in front of my very eyes. Things like that just made the seven years gallop by, as if they had all merged into one gloriously fast, rich, adventurous one.

Yet now, as I sat with Shimon and Elizabeth together with their little ones sound asleep, I could see that so much had happened with life outside of my Jerusalem bubble. The three little ones nestled in Shimon and Elizabeth's laps made me realise that I needed to resign myself to the fact that Sarah, too, must now also have a family of her own. Even though I smiled and thanked my hosts for their welcome, once more I felt alone. Isolated and deeply, deeply lonely.

I waited for a few days in their home and didn't venture out. To be honest, I was frightened. But that's not quite an accurate description: I was petrified. I feared Saul and what he would do if he caught up with me. His gang of temple guards had no mercy, and witnessing such hatred as I had done in the synagogue made it very hard to sleep. Whenever I remembered murder of Stephen and Joseph, I became paralysed with terror. I cried going to bed each night and, through my tears, I had one prayer: 'Mighty Jesus, come and give me strength. Speak to me and lead me."

"This is the time Jesus spoke to you about. He has called you to be an evangelist." I didn't stir.

"Excuse me," the voice said once more, firmly. Followed by a sound of two loud claps, the kind you would use to scare an animal away. "This is the time

Jesus spoke to you about. He has called you to be an evangelist."

Hearing it for the second time I woke up, squinting my eyes still remembering the vibrant light that caused me to shield them in my dream. In the dream the angel spoke like echoing rivers flowing deep into my chest. It had caused me to reach for breath through the intensity of the feeling. It was overwhelming. As I came around I could hardly breathe. I opened my eyes from the dream, but the bright light remained, despite it being the middle of the night. Pitch dark was everywhere apart from in the corner of the room where there stood a large figure surrounded in white. White, intense light that only filled the corner of the room while the rest remained in darkness.

"Did you hear me?" he asked. His accent was northern, yet gentle like a farmer. Nonetheless his form wasn't that of a lowly farmer but rather a soldier. I nodded. And with that he smiled and he simply said, "Good."

The intense light slowly faded, as did he.

Over breakfast I looked for an opportunity to tell Shimon the dream, but I couldn't get a word in edgewise, as they wanted to tell me more about the past seven years, with great enthusiasm. Besides, the bread was still warm and especially tasty with the lavish offering of oil and dried figs that Elizabeth served with it. I was so engrossed in eating the delicious breakfast and thinking about the vision or dream that I had experienced during the night that I didn't listen properly to what Shimon and Elizabeth were enthusing about. I only caught the tail-end of Shimon's monologue, which ended with a question that made my heart race and my chest tighten instantly.

"...So, would you like me to introduce you when you preach in the market square?" he asked coolly.

Without knowing anything about it, Shimon had already sent word out and about in the town that I would be speaking. Me, speaking!

"You want me to do what?!" I shouted, bits of bread and dried fruit flying out my mouth towards Shimon and Elizabeth as they reclined were we ate. Their smiles remained, as if my reaction was a joke. They both laughed and continued to do so as they grabbed their outer garments and sandals, ready to venture into the heart of the town.

They waited patiently by the gate, holding the hands of their children as I remained seated on the smooth courtyard floor. Eventually I managed to make my way up and follow after them, close behind, as the children laughed and played along the way. I didn't say a word. I couldn't. I wanted to run but Shimon had shared with the town that I would be speaking.

Thomas and I were, in a strange way, town legends from the last time we had visited, when Jesus had trained us and sent us out seven years ago!

My hands felt strangely heavy. Very heavy. We met a few fellow believers in the market square, though I don't remember their names. I hadn't met anyone else over the three days of hiding away in Shimon's home, and meeting new people felt overwhelming.

My heart was beating fast, my mouth dry, it was the first time I had preached in public and I started to come up with excuses and reasons in my mind why I couldn't. How could I tell Shimon that what they were expecting me to do would be the first time since I had stood before the Seventy Two, all those years ago. All the years I lived and served in Jerusalem as a disciple and Deacon I hadn't spoken publicly. Not once.

The sky was clear apart from one cloud that hung like an observer to the right of the market. It was strangely pure white, oval and still. The weather was scorching and the lack of a breeze didn't help. I was sweating, both from the heat and nerves. Soon a good crowd gathered around us, perhaps one hundred people, but I wasn't really counting as I couldn't look around. I felt physically sick and feared that, if I did scan the crowds, I would throw up in front of them. The more I sat feeling sick, the more the crowd seemed to grow.

10. Our Meeting

Shimon gave an exuberant introduction and explanation that it was I, alongside Thomas, who was the first person to have brought the message and teachings of Jesus to the city. By the time he had finished 'bigging me up', two to three hundred more people had joined the crowd.

I scanned the back for a quick getaway and saw that the market square was jam-packed. There was only a small gap, just big enough for people to squeeze between the stalls and the rear of the crowd for those who had no interest in listening, or who had to get somewhere.

With the help of Shimon hoisting me up by my elbow, I stood on an old crate in front of the crowd. A hush moved out across all of them and I caught the eyes of some of those whom I vaguely recognised – people who had been healed all those years ago. They nodded and smiled, and this calmed my nerves quickly. Yet, after what seemed like an age of standing with everyone's eyes fixed on me, I knew it was time to open my mouth. I used the sleeve of my garment to wipe away the beads of sweet on my forehead and spoke. What flowed somewhat surprised me: "My friends, you have all heard of the power of Jesus over sickness and evil spirits, look around you and see those who have been made well."

I paused as the crowd looked around them to see the dozen or so people who they had known before being healed, who were now well – standing shoulder to shoulder with those gathered. I pointed at some. A few gave a little wave and as they looked around them and met the glances of others who, in turn, gave reassuring smiles. Before I could continue, one ear-splitting shriek followed another, five or six, each one louder than the previous as evil spirits fled from people stood in the crowd. Not only were the people identified by their cries but also from small circles that formed around the screaming people in the throng as those near them stepped and jumped back.

Each circle in the crowd revealed a bewildered looking man or women.

"I'm free!" someone shouted.

Another, who had not been able to speak since birth, started to proclaim praises to the Lord. It was a strange melody and sounded dry and raspy, but the more she praised the Lord, the clearer it became.

I glanced down at my arms and despite the heat of the day I pushed my sleeves up and saw that goose bumps had formed. I shuddered at the intensity of the presence of heaven in the market square and, like my dream encounter with the angel, I found it almost hard to breathe. Yet with every breath I struggled to exhale I felt Jesus walk amongst the crowds by his Spirit and tenderly touch and reach out to those who stood gathered to hear me. It was utterly beautiful to see him, yet not physically, but spiritually mingle shoulder to shoulder one moment in the crowd and then fly like a dove the next, descending on the hungry people who had gathered to hear the 'famous' Philip.

I smiled as I stood before the crowd, but then a thought made me panic inside. If this was what happened within one sentence of proclaiming the gospel, this whole city is going to be turned upside down in five minutes! With that thought I dared to continue.

"His name is so powerful, as you can see. I mean, look at what happens when 'Jesus' is mentioned!" Three more shrieks echoed around the market square. Many in the crowd looked around nervously but some people laughed at the precise timing.

The old lady who had been sitting in the market for as long as anyone in Beth Shean could remember raised her hands and, as she stood, she shouted: "Excuse me, young man!" in a strong, clear voice. She hoisted herself upon an old wooden box. She wore a long brown outer garment which had many, many other shades of brown with layers of dirt from the market, and she pointed at me and called out once more. From where I stood I saw the crowd strain to see who it was that was calling out. They all turned to the right of the crowd where she had always sat, propped up against the remains of an old well wall. Within a few moments a wave of explanation rippled through the crowd as people passed on who it was who was shouting. People strained even more to see the woman that no-one had ever heard speak before. Ever.

Every day, for as long as people could remember, she had sat in the market with her begging bowl, not even acknowledging the kindness of those who gave her bread or a few coins. She simply couldn't talk and no-one even knew who put her out in the market at the beginning of the day or who it was that collected her once the market had closed up at sunset.

The crowd hushed, as it had done when I had stood up a few minutes previously, but instead of looking at me, everyone was now straining to hear what the woman, whom no one had ever heard speak before, had to say.

"Excuse me young man!" she said again. Her voice wasn't harsh, rather it sounded pleasing, velvety and kind. "Can you please tell me, what is this all over me?" Astonished, she looked behind her and held her arms before her and at the same time gazed below and on top of them, trying to see what it was, "what is this sweetness upon me?" she enquired.

I spoke directly to her, eyes fixed upon hers. They were radiant yet looked puzzled and almost frightened. I spoke above the heads of those who watched, possessed with a clarity and boldness that I didn't quite understand. But, as I spoke, I liked the sound and also the feel of the words that seemed to flow naturally from me. It felt good, like well-crafted keys that had the ability to open the most stubborn of old locks.

"I've got some great news to share with you, sister. The untameable, unapproachable, all holy God who is beyond our very grasp... He is right here! It is he that that you feel upon you. The good news is that you, me, each one of us can now be forgiven for our sins and have a close relationship with the creator of the earth and the heavens!"

The crowd's attention fixed upon me and the old woman as the preach became a strange engagement between the two of us with a few hundred people eavesdropping.

"But, how can this happen?" The woman shouted.

"Let me explain," I beamed confidently.

"The last time I was here in this city, the message I brought was about the kingdom of heaven coming. Now I have more to add to this message. The signs you see, feel and hear are pointers to show you that what I bring is true! God gave his Son to each one of us, he laid down his life as a perfect, spotless sacrifice. It is through him that we can now have direct access to God who we can now call: Abba Father!" I raised my hands as if clasping hold of a hand of a tall dad standing next to me.

The woman also raised her hands as I spoke and waved them around like branches swaying in the breeze. Strange as it was, her actions didn't seem out of place and at that moment a few others also waved and uttered words of praise silently.

I continued, "Jesus, who is God's Son, is the only one who has died and has come back to life. After three days he rose again from the grave, proving that he also has power over death! The greatest miracle of all is that he offers us a new life, to turn from all that we know is wrong and to live under his rule. I plead with you today: make Jesus your king!" I shouted it again: "Make Jesus your king! He offers purpose. He offers an adventure beyond our wildest dreams, and this is to each one of us if we choose to follow him."

As I looked at the woman I felt that same gentle warmth upon my chest that I had felt all those years previously when I met Jesus in the market in Jerusalem with the taste of the grape still fresh in my mouth. It was as if, like then, he was placing his hand upon my chest.

I felt him speak: 'Her name is Martha.' Without pausing to think whether it really was her name or not I called, "Martha! Will you turn from your sin and follow Jesus today?"

She stood motionless and with her mouth open. Then she cried aloud:

"You know my name!" She held her hands close to her chest. Her face shone as she smiled. "He knows my name!" she said once more turning to those immediately around her, yet the whole crowd had heard her.

The story of the 'old beggar woman' had spread across the town in a few minutes and more people had gathered, wanting to see her.

She repeated the phrase 'He knows my name' over and over. No-one in the whole of the city had ever known her name, and when the crowd heard me call it there was a kind of tangible intake of breath that could be heard like one, right across the market.

I heard someone near the front whisper, "The beggar has a name."

Slowly rippling throughout the crowd, people started to clap and a cheer. This built up until a crescendo of noise filled the market square. From where I stood I saw a dozen or so people push their way to the front of where I had been speaking and one by one they knelt right by me. Martha had also made

205

the journey, fighting through the crowds, unstable on her legs that had never worked before, and she was helped to the front. As she bowed her head near to where I stood, I could still hear her utter "He knows my name," over and over.

Her tears made dark patches and lines down her filthy garment. I stood looking at it for a while, fascinated by the random patterns that the tears made. I then looked at the growing line of men and women kneeling, and instinctively walked, slowly along, praying for each one and placing my hands upon them as they repented from their sins and prayed to make Jesus their king.

One after the other I prayed. Instead of the line getting shorter, it grew. More and more people joined the line for prayer and soon it snaked all around the perimeter of the market square. There were even some people kneeling and waiting to be prayed for who hadn't heard me speak, but had heard from family members my message as they approached the market. Coupled with seeing the miracle of those they had previously known to be sick completely made well, they felt compelled to respond to the message I brought.

It was after a few hours, when I started feeling very tired even with the help and support of Shimon and Elizabeth, that I got to the last one kneeling in the pale dirt. Her head was bowed low and, like most who came for prayer, she was weeping. She had one of the most colourfully embroidered patterns around the neck of her outer garment. Part of it caught my eye. It was the same fish emblem as mine, only it was interlaid with another. For a moment, I looked at the pattern and then looked at my own on the outer garment. Its similarity was striking.

As I laid my hands upon her head to pray, all I could think about was whether she had heard of my Sarah. I hoped that somehow she had, and had bought it from her and could tell me where she was.

At the 'amen' she looked up.

It was her.

With my hand still on her head, I stood rooted to the spot. Not sure as to what to say she gently took my hand from atop her head and pulled it down to her side, clasping it. Holding her hand felt like home once more. She stood still holding it and, with the other, she gently wiped the tears that now rolled down my face.

"I missed you too," she said.

Then, before I could try and explain or say anything, she smiled and looked deeply into my eyes. Her brown beautiful eyes that I had dreamed of over and over throughout the seven years in Jerusalem danced reassuringly as I looked deeply into them.

"I've waited for you," she said.

Our meeting was interrupted as I was ushered away to the other side of the market by two women who showed me where a man had collapsed and was shaking uncontrollably.

"Please come, Philip. They need you to pray."

Someone added, "We don't know what's going on." Even though didn't know, either, I obediently went with them and left Sarah standing where she had been prayed for.

I tried explaining to the women that this was all new to me too as I walked over to the far end of the market square where the man lay on the ground, shaking.

"Shall I call for the doctor?" called a concerned market worker. I explained that we would wait and see what had happened and I gently spoke to the shaking man on the ground, who by now was also groaning and looking all around him, alarmed. When he saw me crouch beside him, he wriggled even more and tried to get away, as if I would harm him.

Someone fetched a goblet of wine for him and two of us managed to sit him on a step to talk with him. He could only utter four words over and over, and his hands continued shaking as he held the dark red earthen goblet.

"I've met with God."

It turned out that his wife had sent him out to fetch some flour and fruit in the market and as he entered the square he had become overwhelmed with the presence of God and had lost all control of his limbs and had fallen under a weight.

"God spoke to me and told me that I needed to change and live for him," he humbly whispered. He also became a follower of Jesus and joined the growing Beth Shean church that day.

After praying for the man who had an encounter with God in the market, Shimon stepped next to me and assumed the role of big brother and guard. After a long first day of praying for people and praying for healing for numerous men, women and children, he walked with his arm around me and ushered me back to his home for something to eat and some rest too. As he led me away, I glanced around, scanning the scene of the small groups of people still huddled around the market in the dusk and looked, longing for one more glimpse of Sarah. But I couldn't see her.

"I didn't imagine it, did I, Shimon?" I asked. I was worried that somehow meeting Sarah had been some weird dream or vision.

"Imagine that amazing outpouring of the Spirit and all those people experiencing new life?! No, that really happened my friend," Shimon enthused.

"I know, I know..." I quickly replied, somewhat irritably. "I mean meeting Sarah... she was there, right, wasn't she, Shimon?" Panic began to rise in my chest as I feared that in my nervousness I had somehow become delusional.

"Do not fear, my brother." Shimon placed his big arm around me as we walked back to his place. "Why don't you invite her for a meal here tomorrow evening, and you two can catch up properly." As he said this, he stopped and turned to look at me face to face. "God is good, Philip. Remember, he has a great plan for your life!"

Later that evening I confided in Shimon that it had been my very first public announcing of the good news, ever. It had resulted in over seventy men and women making a commitment to follow Jesus, with a further twenty or so asking if they could find out more. Shimon laughed. "Why didn't you say so, Philip?" he said, shaking his head in unbelief. "I tried, Shimon, believe me I tried! But you thought I was joking!"

After I had had something to eat and drink and given thanks to the Lord for all that he had done in Beth Shean, I wrote a prayer that was like a poem.

It was hurried, written in the candlelight, but it captured how I felt. It had been a harrowing week: from escaping from imprisonment and certain death in the custody of Saul to an outbreak of the Spirit in the market square!

I had found that Jesus had clearly gone before me. In having to flee Jerusalem, I met Jesus afresh. He was already at work in this city and watching him love and lavish his power upon those who eagerly gathered in the town made me even more in awe of him than before.

Sitting in my small room in Shimon's home I began to really believe for the first time that Jesus had chosen me. For seven years I had grappled with the idea that he would call someone like me, and now I was beginning to believe that he really did want to use me powerfully for his fame, and so that others too may experience the gift of his life for theirs.

Following you

My heart feels like it might burst, like it is on fire!

I did it! Yes, I finally opened my mouth and spoke about you and what you have done.

Your call upon me, I so much admire

That you would choose someone slight like me

To usher in something so huge, to allow me to follow in your slipstream, to go further and higher

I want to glorify you Lord Jesus and show your
power and your grace
To show your kingdom that is coming more and
more each day
I want to serve you with all I've got, I want to
see your face.
Thank you for bringing me to this town once
more
To meet my best friend again and see you at
work,
I can't wait to go on this new adventure with
you and kingdom explore.
Thank you my friend, my Saviour. Amen.

It felt like the whole town was filled with joy through
the message that we had brought. But it was the signs
and wonders that the Lord did to prove that what I
said was true that truly showed his power and
goodness.

I too was filled with delight! Meeting Sarah again
and hearing her kind words felt like this really was an
opportunity of regaining my best friend, but also
regaining my confidence. The overshadowing lack of
self-assurance in my call that I had carried for so long
was dissipating, alongside the sense of being
abandoned. I felt at home once more.

11

Our Marriage

AD 37, 23 years old

Shimon and Elizabeth gave their home for the party. It lasted for three days, with some time for sleep and replenishing the food in the small hours in-between. The food was good and the wine even better, but it was the joy and goodness in the atmosphere that kept people lingering.

Intermingled with the dancing and music we sang songs of praise. Those we had met in the preparations for the wedding, as we fetched food and wine, were quickly invited and, alongside family and friends, strangers found a seat at the feast!

It was a celebration where those you would least expect were welcome. Someone mentioned that it was like an illustration of one of the stories from Jesus. The wedding banquet where the servants went out into the highways and byways and looked for people to invite. Strangers became friends and were well fed and treated generously with the delicious wine that Shimon and his family provided – from a friend's vineyard who wanted to give the wine. Why? He too had been healed at the market the first time I dared to speak publicly.

Mum looked radiant and not surprisingly danced the most. By far. Judas joined her in the celebrations. He had since taken mum as his new wife and he looked like a new person; beard neatly trimmed, it took ten years off him, as did his new clean clothes and a thankful, handsome smile. He had moved into our home under mum's persuasion. She had insisted on installing a large wash area in the yard so that he could bathe and clean after his hard days' work at the tanning yard.

I tried sending word to my dad. At great expense, I managed to find someone who was heading for Rome to deliver a letter, but it was almost impossible to know where he lived. And even though I had enquired of every visitor from Rome who ventured into our small village, my investigations drew a blank. He might already have died.

Sarah and I rented a little home a few minutes' walk from the market square. It felt fitting to be so close to the place we had been reacquainted. Our home had a dark red door. The mantle was low and wonky and Sarah loved to fill the broken earthen wine-vat that stood proudly outside with wild flowers. It kind of compensated for the irregular angles and badly fitting door that didn't quite fill the entrance. Towards the back we had a small yard, and in the corner we planted a peach tree, a wedding gift from Shimon and Elizabeth. It was only as tall as me, but we hoped that it too would be as fruitful as theirs and become a summer treat.

Our bed was a gift from my mum and Judas. It was adorned with the most beautiful leather work, patterns of hearts and stars on each side and along the top. Sarah had filled our home with the most beautiful handicraft and across the doorway to our bedroom was a long red drape on which she had embroidered white flowers.

Once all the guests had left the wedding feast, we were ushered away to our new home and we didn't leave our beautiful bedroom for a full day. We slept and made love and talked and prayed until our hunger got the better of us and I ventured to the market for some bread and fruit.

The town felt new. It was lighter, more so easy to breathe. People seemed to walk with their heads held high, greeting and smiling at each other, when before they seemed somewhat suspicious of one another.

Over the months that we lived in the centre of the town, most people had the opportunity to hear the good news of Jesus and the new start that he offered. Of course, there were some who refused to listen and didn't want to talk, but the overwhelming majority of people in that town had heard the good news and well over half had decided to give their lives to Jesus. But it wasn't just me who was the preacher or teacher, I couldn't take all the credit. While on most days we would meet in the market square, others had taken initiative and invited people to their homes, where large numbers of people gathered to eat and hear of the miracles that Jesus had done in the city.

The town was filled with more and more groups of people who would meet to pray together early in the morning and throughout the day. Singing, laughing and praying could be heard across the city, when before there was none. It was as if it bubbled over and out of people's homes. No one planned it or orchestrated it. It just happened.

People who had fallen out with each other were reunited and sought forgiveness. The city felt like it had ascended upon a mountain, as the air was lighter and sweet to breathe. Visitors to the town would comment about the atmosphere. Meals were long and felt less about eating and more about lingering with one another and enjoying company.

Children played in the streets when before they were kept inside their homes for fear of those who would harm them. Possessions were naturally shared, to a ridiculous level. The man who had been homeless and begging near the court found a new home with the magistrate who dressed him in fine clothes and treated him like a brother.

After our wedding celebrations, I was advised to take time off to be with Sarah. We enjoyed a peaceful few weeks in our new home. Time to talk, eat and walk together. And of course, to swim.

It was my first day back and feeling refreshed that I was asked to help by fetching some food for a visiting team that included some of the original Jesus followers. I walked alone, humming a quiet song, when I was stopped. In my tracks. He blocked the narrow path that led under the low stone archway to the market square. His form silhouetted against the bright entrance to the square. The traders and hubbub of bargaining and laughter echoed through the archway behind him.

I stepped to the side. He copied. Whenever I moved to the right or left he stood to block the way. After a dozen or so times I laughed and smiling I declared, "Hey, we make a good dance duo!"

His response wasn't quite what I was expecting and he growled: "I'm someone great. I am to be feared!"

He stepped closer to square up to me, but instead of looking eye to eye I had to strain to look up. His chiselled features showed scars and dents. It was clear that he was well used to fighting. He was around my age, had dark brown hair and a curious scar that travelled from the right of his forehead down to his cheek that somehow also travelled down over his eye brow and lid.

"I'm the great power of God!" he announced.

"Seriously?" I said. "The great power of God?" I started to laugh and this irritated him and he grabbed the front of my tunic and lifted me up, causing me to stand on tip toes as he breathed upon my face.

I continued. "I've met with the living God and he is nothing like you. He is humble. He even washed the feet of his friends! You're no power of God. You're arrogant. Compared with what I know, you're just full of ox dung."

And with that he lowered me down. And even though I half expected a beating, he let me walk by.

I blinked in the bright light of the market and checked behind me to still see, in the shadows, the man standing and shaking his head. He was soon walking behind me but not aggressively or menacingly. From that hour, Simon followed me like a lost puppy. I must admit I had a twinge of guilt for being so harsh with him, but I had heard of his magic tricks before. It was a just a matter of time until the dark powers that he used would cause him and me to collide and I knew this was an opportunity for Jesus to rescue someone that many had written off as beyond the pale of being part of the new church.

I guess I had become impatient when it came down to the devil's con-tricks. I had met way too many people who had lived most of their lives under the miserable lies of the devil and, while they were now living in the abundance of the life that Jesus brings, they also carried a sense of regret that they hadn't heard of the truth earlier and had spent many years living like slaves to lies. I knew how this felt, having believed that I was useless, abandoned. Worthless.

Simon didn't say anything for a few days, but wherever I went serving the church in Beth Shean he watched. Even when I worked alongside Sarah and Shimon praying for the sick and proclaiming Jesus as the Christ, Simon would be watching from a safe distance.

As a team, we also washed people's feet as we prayed over them. It was this that seemed to vex him the most and I would often look up and see him pace the ground and shake furiously whenever we did.

One day after a day's walk, we met a family in the village and we offered to wash their feet, including those of the three young children. As Simon watched, he spoke up and asked me a question. It wasn't what I was expecting.

As I crouched down cleaning out the bowl of water, Simon tapped me on my shoulder. I turned to look up at him. He had red, puffy eyes from crying, but had tried to hide it.

With an intensely pained expression he stated, "Philip, I have watched you for nearly two weeks now. I used to think that I was great, but now I know I am nothing. What you have is real. My power was just magic and tricks. Would you please wash my feet? Please. I need you to wash them as a sign that I now believe in your Jesus and will follow him, like you."

"Are you really ready to believe in Jesus as the Messiah and to make him your king?" I asked.

With his head bowed, the tears he had so desperately tried to hide fell again from his face as he nodded.

After we had washed his feet and prayed for him, Simon grabbed the bowl and towel and did something so unusual it took me surprise. He stood in the middle of the small village market square with his hands held aloft and his eyes looking towards the fading sky. The few market stall holders were packing away their wares under the bright covered canopies that had sheltered the tables and bowls of dried fruit and nuts. And there Simon stood, in the large bowl that we had just used to wash his feet. At first I was concerned that it would break and indicated to him that he should get out. But the crowds started to gather, much like when I had spoken for the first time back in Beth Shean. He stood by a raised wall. A well had once stood there but was now covered and piles of weathered rocks and created a focal point in the centre of the village.

Simon's reputation of performing great signs was known throughout the region and soon the crowd grew much stronger. Some carrying their shopping in their arms stopped, others had abandoned their stalls to see what tricks he was going to perform.

With a loud voice that filled the four corners of the market he announced: "I am Simon the sorcerer! You have heard that I have great powers! You know that I can perform great tricks!"

The crowd hushed and every eye was upon him, attentive to what he was going to do. Young children were lifted upon shoulders so that they too could enjoy the show.

Then he screamed: "Do you want to see something amazing?!"

The crowd cheered, and before I was able to stop him from whatever idiotic thing he had planned, he asked the question again and again as he worked the crowd like a true showman and whipped them up in excitement. They cheered louder and louder. He then declared with his hands aloft: "Then watch this!"

And with that, he knelt down. Beside the wall of the old well and out of the sight of the crowds had sat a beggar. He had been unnoticed due to his dirty clothes that had blended in with the brown wall and somehow this camouflaged him with the old well. That, coupled with the fact that he was very much 'part of the furniture' of this market square and had sat in the market for as long as anyone could remember. This made him almost invisible to most.

Simon quietly asked the man some questions and then proceeded to wash his feet, delicately and slowly. People strained to see what he was doing on the ground and pushed to peer through. Many manoeuvred and shifted as much as they could to see what he was doing. The crowd started murmuring sharing what they saw and, after a few minutes, word had spread as one told another what he was doing. Simon stood up.

In a low voice that caused the chattering crowd to stop still, Simon gently said, "I am really not great. Today I have met with the Messiah, our long-awaited Saviour, and I have chosen to follow him. His name is Jesus and he has freely laid down his life for me and for you. He died as a perfect sacrifice to take our punishment. On the third day, he rose again to prove that he was the Son of the living God!"

His retelling of the gospel was clear, and as he spoke I marvelled as to how he managed to communicate something so much clearer than how I had told him.

People listened intently as he continued, "Now I have washed the feet of this man here as a symbol of what Jesus can do for each one of us. He longs to wash us and make us new. We also can believe and be baptised into a new way of life." And then he said something that I wasn't ready for: "Here's my new friend Philip, who told me about Jesus, to explain some more." He pointed at me and indicated that I should make my way through the crowds to also come up and speak.

It was fairly easy to connect with the crowd as they had been astonished by Simon. I explained the free gift of God's grace. Of Jesus. Of him being given for each one of us and how being baptised was a sign of what Jesus can do inside each one of us. With the sun setting, twenty six people – men, women and children – followed us down to the river to be baptised and give their lives to following King Jesus.

The long journey back home the following day to Beth Shean felt like a gentle stroll as we reflected on all that the Lord had done in our midst. Plans were made to start a church meeting in people's homes and Sarah and I promised to visit with Simon again to teach the emerging church.

Peter and John, some of the first friends of Jesus, heard of all the miracles that the Lord was doing in the city and region of Samaria and came to visit Sarah and me.

When they arrived, they wanted to know everything that had happened since I fled Jerusalem. We gathered in the largest homes of the disciples, those owned by the magistrates. Together we spent time marvelling at all the Lord had done and I explained that, even though people had been dramatically healed and also delivered from evil spirits, I hadn't managed to pray for people to receive the Holy Spirit like I had seen people do in Jerusalem. I explained that I longed to see others operate in his gifts and power.

"We can sort that one out!" John said with a cheeky smile.

"It's well strange," Peter continued, "whenever we lay hands on people The Spirit falls upon them and in them. Whoooosh!" and with that he laughed waving his hands like a river in front of him.

John continued speaking as Peter carried on waving his hands, much to the children's delight. He looked funny with his arms and hands moving. Bobbing up and down as if in a fast-moving river.

"It's amazing, really. We're not sure why he chooses us to share in his power, but one thing we know for sure, people are the most amazing conductors of him! I can promise you that when we pray for you and the team you also will be able to impart him. And all the gifts that he chooses to give people, well they will just bubble open in them."

As John continued to explain the gifts of the Spirit, more of the disciples drew away from the table of food and drew close to hear what he had to say. Among the crowd gathered was Simon. He had joined the growing team who were doing the works of Jesus in and around the city. Despite his height and build, which made me look like a midget in comparison, I had become like his bigger brother, and I was so grateful for the opportunity to train and help someone in the faith to do what I did as an evangelist. I wanted him to have everything that I had as a growing evangelist. And he was doing so well in learning how to introduce people to Jesus and also learn about him, too. Well, that is, apart from the day John and Peter came to stay.

As part of John's illustration, he asked for volunteers, and he and Peter began to pray for those eager to experience the indwelling of the Spirit. The people who came forward were all new believers, some a few days old in their faith, others part of the first crowd in the market when I first spoke in Beth Shean.

When Simon saw Peter and John laying their hands on people to receive the Holy Spirit and when he saw tongues of fire fall upon their heads, feeling the rush of wind as he fell upon them, his eyes became round as silver platters and I knew what must have been going through his head.

"Calm down, Simon." I whispered to him. "Just watch and enjoy what the Lord is doing...."

But he couldn't contain his enthusiasm and, after Peter had prayed for the new believers and with some still laying upon the ground overwhelmed by the power of the Spirit, Simon asked if he too could have the gift of laying on of hands. Without giving Peter an opportunity to respond, he even offered them some money to *buy* the gift, holding out his pouch of silver coins.

The loud rebuke was shocking.

Peter tore into him: "Oi! How dare you! You can't buy this s gift! It's not for sale, you idiot! You know what? Your heart is not right before God, now repent or you will perish with your stupid money!"

Simon fell on his knees and sobbed. I pulled him up and whispered "I told you, brother, just watch. You get too excited, Simon."

Every one of the 15 days after the apostles arrived was full. From dawn to dusk it was relentless. I needed some time away. I loved how more and more people were travelling in to experience the outpouring of the Spirit, but the crowds made me tired. The Holy Spirit set people free and met them right where they were – all kinds of people: beggars on the street to town officials had met with the Spirit. And while I would never grow tired of how any who were willing were impacted by the outpouring, I valued my alone time. I was simply exhausted by God's pace. I needed some space.

There's no doubt that he is a genius at what he does: the Spirit multiplied the ministry of Jesus from one side of the town to the other. There were stories of people simultaneously being healed on the same evening in different homes. As if this wasn't hard enough to try to get my head around, one night we heard of a nearby town that was also experiencing an outpouring and people were dramatically healed. Trying to fathom this was hard. I had seen Jesus with my own eyes deal with people in the most powerful ways, but it was always one after the other. One place. One time. One person at a time. Granted, I had never seen Jesus turn anyone away, but his impact was always within the confines of a time and place. My head ached as I thought about how he was then and watching him at work now, through his Spirit. Same Jesus, but multiplied over and over.

The Spirit seemed to be turning up everywhere and at first this panicked me. I wondered whether this was something that could be genuine, or if people were simply copying the signs and manifestations of the Spirit that they had seen in others. But the healing still happened left, right and centre and I reasoned that the Spirit really can appear at different places at the same time.

I remembered the words of Jesus when he taught us about another counsellor coming, one who would do greater things and lead us into all truth. It's true. His Spirit was so mightily at work in Samaria. Every day, for fifteen days on the trot, we saw one person after another being filled with the Spirit and encountering Jesus. Dramatic miracles took place, a young man close to my age had died two days previously and was brought back to life after Peter had prayed for him. His parents had already laid on an elaborate funeral. A young girl who had never spoken or heard received her speech and hearing when I placed my hands upon her head. Her mum was so overcome and filled with the Spirit that she shook and cried for over 24 hours as he fell upon her.

I needed some time alone. To pray and clear my mind from the hubbub and excitement. To be still.

Sarah understood and, as I explained what I needed to do, she listened and packed up a picnic and sent me off for a few hours at the end of a busy day to walk alone and take some deep breaths.

I walked down towards the old market, now at the end of the day it was deserted. The colourful awnings that hung in front of the sun-bleached tables fluttered in the gentle breeze like large children's kites, tamed by wooden poles on each side.

There was a large, solitary man sitting by one of the fruit stalls, watching me approach. I adjusted the angle of my walk so as not to walk right by him. I didn't want to be recognised. The sunlight behind him glowed and while any other man would be silhouetted by it, it was as if the rays where shining right through him. Like he was made of glass. I sheltered my eyes as I drew a bit closer, meaning to walk on past him to the other side of the square without saying a word – let alone staring at this bulky figure leaning against an old wall. His sheer size made me think of gladiator or soldier but his face was very kind and strangely welcoming. His countenance was definitely not one that could be associated with fighting or war.

"Go down to the desert road, the one that leads to Gaza," he called out in a monotone. His words sounded like a river rushing over rocks, powerfully strong yet all at the same pitch.

I stopped. "Excuse me?" I said.

"I said, go down to the desert road, the one that leads to Gaza." Again I heard his words, but this time I felt them more. They rushed through me like water falls between your fingers as you scoop to drink with your hands. Each word fell right through my very being and I sensed this deeply within me, like cold living water, but not upon the surface of my skin, rather I felt his words within me.

I tried to question what he was saying and look into his face where he sat, but I had to squint and instead of saying anything I held up my hand to shield my eyes from his bright countenance. His face literally shone. Gold flecks mixed in with the brown flesh of his rugged face and, while I saw stubble and some small scars, it was clear that this man really wasn't a man at all. He opened his mouth and with each word bright light shone from it, as if a small fire was blazing deep within.

"I've been sent to instruct you to leave right now, down to the desert road. Now go."

And with that, he stood. He was enormous yet his height didn't frighten me and, as he reached out his hand towards me, rather than stepping back I somehow instinctively stepped in to receive what he needed to give me. I lifted my head to look squarely up at his face. His hand on my shoulder sent a burning sensation deep down the right side of body. Each burning pulse like that of a heart filled me with power, and as it did I bravely stared deeply into his striking eyes, refusing to pull away from the pulses of power I was receiving.

Within his brown and golden eyes were mysteries, distant lands and a kindness of a father that I had also seen when Jesus breathed upon me and spoke of my call as an evangelist. His eyes also carried sadness, like the eyes of an older man who has seen way too much pain, yet they also looked like the eyes of a new-born child seeing for the first time. Deeply innocent and drinking in their environment. He didn't say another word as he stood with his hand upon my shoulder. He didn't need to. I knew that it was pointless to argue about going. All I needed to do was obey.

But then I thought of Sarah and, like a thump to the stomach that winds, the thought of leaving her took the powerful encounter and transformed it into a deep ache in my chest. Surely I couldn't leave her again? I dropped my gaze from his and looked down at my dusty feet. The ground around the market stall was littered with bits of rotten fruit trodden deeply into the dust, making colourful smears around my feet from the day's trading, rotten brown splodges mixed with those from previous ones. I looked up again to ask him how I would be able to leave Sarah and go, but no one was there. He had gone.

I stood for a while, rooted to the spot. The sensation of warmth carried on pouring down my right side as I thought through the instruction and mapped in my mind the best route to travel to Gaza and then also the simple walk back home to Sarah.

"But what about Sarah?" I spoke out loud into the air. It was then that the Spirit of Jesus spoke into my being.

"Everything is going to be alright, Philip. Now go down to the Gaza road and I will show you how to bring good news to an entire nation. Now go! You need to run."

"Please let her understand," I pleaded into the air as I walked away from the market. Away from my home. Away from my Sarah. "Please speak to her about the instructions that you've given me..." With each step away from her I felt more foolish, so I ran even faster towards the road that led to Gaza. With each breath out, a cry emerged. It was as if I was mourning, and each step and gasp sounded like one of the professional mourners at funerals who would wail and weep, false tears streaming down their faces. Only mine weren't false. Each step took me further away from Sarah and the place that I felt truly alive. Yet, obediently I ran, even though I didn't want to and the further away from our new home I went the deeper the pain in my chest and throat became.

Darkness enveloped me as I continued to run in obedience and even though I couldn't see properly, I carried on. It felt like madness but I knew that I needed to keep going under the instruction I had received.

Goose bumps kept covering my body and as soon as they receded I would remember the angel's words once more and this helped the pain-filled decision of leaving all that I knew as safe and homely and love-filled. Yet there really was only one response to Jesus. I was walking in it.

When I fell and grazed my knees I stopped where I had fallen and lay on the ground. Exhausted, I slept. When I woke, I was covered in dew, sparkling all over me like a shimmering blanket. I was also very warm. The cold dew didn't match the warmth inside me and for a few puzzled minutes I looked closely at the droplets on my arms and legs. Gazing closely through them I could see the world magnified and rounded, the droplets causing the road and sky to merge and glimmer.

It was as I gazed through the droplets on my hand I saw what appeared to be a steam-like haze emerging from two white horses. They pulled a white chariot and in their efforts and within the cool of the morning

I could see their breath puffing from their nostrils and a mist floated off the warmth of their backs. They looked ghostly and elegant.

As I watched, I heard the Spirit speak again. Eight words. But it felt as if he spoke volumes. About nations, destinies of kings and the future of tens upon tens of thousands. All this was breathed through me and as they were ushered into my very being the eight words energised me once more and I didn't need to respond to him. My deep breath became the answer as I readied myself to go, and my body shook involuntarily and so, so violently. For a moment, I stood quaking and laughing, marvelling as the dewdrops spun off me like I was a wet, stray dog.

As the droplets were spiralling they created a circle of wet around me. I shook in the excitement of the words that the Spirit uttered.

"Go to that chariot and stay near it." Eight simple words, but they were full of life and promise. The closer I got, the more I questioned what was I meant to do when I reached it.

It was elegant. White, with gold edges. The horses seemed to effortlessly bounce along rather than trot. They looked graceful. In awe, I looked at the beautiful procession and then looked down at my dusty outer garment. It had a tear on the left that Sarah had been meaning to mend, and approaching the elegant scene I wished she had. This chariot looked too immaculate. It even had royal seals that looked like shields upon it and, the closer I got, the more I saw of the fine detail. The red jewels that were embossed along the top of the carriage twinkled in the rising sunshine and what looked like pineapples shaped into gold proudly stood on the back and front right where the soldiers stood.

Both matched the chariot in their uniform. Spotless white turbans and red vests that revealed enough muscle to indicate that they were not for messing with. They were athletic, soldier-like, one was also the driver of the chariot and he sat at the front while the other guarded the back. The closer I approached, the more incensed he became. And when I ran too close behind the chariot he clasped his sword handle that hung in the scabbard to his side, indicating for me to stay back. Next to him lay a white bow and arrow, the arrows were wooden yet the feathered end was made from pure white quills, the sharp end also white, matching the carriage.

I continued to run as if I needed to somehow get the attention of the person within and with all my might I gave another push to run faster so as to be in parallel with him. The driver brought the horses to a sudden stop and simultaneously reached for his sword and held it pointing in my direction. We stayed frozen for a long moment, him seated and pointing his sword and me standing at the side, hands raised to show I was unarmed. The only movement was the heavy breathing from the horses as they patiently stood awaiting the next command. The man at the back loaded an arrow and took aim at me, stretching the string of the bow back. I didn't see this at first, as the passenger held my attention.

He looked like a woman, yet his clothes were that of a man. And despite his large breasts and womanly smooth face there was no mistaking that he was indeed a man.

He stopped reading out loud. They were sentences that I recognised. He then looked quizzically at his driver and then shouted, irritably.

"Why have we stopped? We need to make good time for me to get back to the palace! Get a move on, man!"

He then turned to see where his driver's gaze was fixed and followed the direction of his sword to where I stood.

I blurted out without a word of introduction, "Do you understand what you're reading?"

"How can I unless I have someone who can help me interpret it?"

He then read out a portion of the scroll again, even though I had heard him read it as I had stood waiting to catch his attention.

"He was despised and rejected by others;
a man of suffering and acquainted with infirmity;
and as one from whom others hide their faces
he was despised, and we held him of no account.
Surely he has borne our infirmities
and carried our diseases;
yet we accounted him stricken,
struck down by God, and afflicted.
But he was wounded for our transgressions,
crushed for our iniquities;
upon him was the punishment that made us whole,
and by his bruises we are healed.
All we like sheep have gone astray;
we have all turned to our own way,
and the Lord has laid on him
the iniquity of us all."

He paused and took a deep breath. With a low voice he then said, "These words are like life to me. They're powerful but I don't understand them." He fixed his gaze upon me and with a smile asked, "Can you tell me, who is this man talking about, himself or someone else? I hope you don't mind me asking you but it's so strange you standing there by my carriage. I was just longing for someone to explain to me what I was reading and here you are! You have the look of a man of honour and you have such a kind face. Would you please help me understand these words?"

I nodded and stepped closer. As I did, the man simply waved his arm and the sword and arrow where lowered and put aside immediately.

"Come and travel with me for a while, you look tired and I could offer you a lift."

Although I smiled at his invitation, inside I wasn't sure about actually travelling with him. I was happy to speak about Jesus from the side of the carriage at a safe distance, but to travel with him was another thing altogether. The carriage was taller than I had expected and I had to look up at the man in his elegant carriage. As I saw him even more clearly, I felt increasingly uncomfortable. The man looked strangely beautiful and as I stood gazing upon him I just couldn't quite understand what I was looking at. The beauty of a dark-skinned woman but also a man. All in one. I had heard of eunuchs before but had never met one, and right now I didn't know whether I liked what I saw or not.

Besides, my Jewish upbringing had taught me that it was taboo for me to spend any time with Gentiles, let alone eunuchs! Samaritans I had gotten used to (useful really, as I was married to one) but to sit beside a Gentile whose role in life was to oversee the beds of the harem for Royalty as they had multiple sex partners made me feel very uncomfortable, and I found it hard to breathe as I stood rooted to the spot, unable to act upon his invitation to join him in the carriage.

Scratching my elbow and then my neck I felt dirty standing so close to the carriage. I stood without saying a word but he smiled and without showing any concern for my awkwardness he simply shuffled along on the seat and patted the pure white fleece that he sat on, indicating for me to join him. I'm pleased that he did that as, to be honest, it was the last thing I wanted to do, yet I felt it strangely right and while breathing a silent prayer to Jesus asking for help I hoisted myself into the carriage and sat beside him. It was large enough to create enough space for us to turn towards each other and continue our conversation and, while we did this, our knees touched and I looked around me for the easiest way to jump straight off. As I turned, the guard placed a golden goblet in my hand. The water was cold and had orange slices within it that jiggled about as the carriage moved with the bumpy road. The water was good and I drank it all, not realising how thirsty the run had made me.

"My name is Philip," I finally said, clumsily introducing myself as the carriage moved along the uneven road towards Gaza. "Thank you for the lift…" I paused, wondering whether to say that I had been instructed by Jesus to find him, but before I could work out how to explain this he asked me that question again. I thought it quite odd that he didn't introduce himself, share his name or explain what he did. It was as if his chariot and soldiers should be obvious enough as to his importance.

He asked: "Tell me, is the writer writing about himself or someone else or someone who has yet to be born?"

"I've got some great news for you, my friend!" I smiled. "I've actually met this person the ancient scroll prophesies about. Truly I have! I have seen him with my very eyes. I've spoken with him, learnt from him and he changed my life. Starting with Jesus, I spoke about his life, how he had healed my mum and how I had met him down by the river where he gave me a fig. I shared the story about Marcus and my attempt to kill him. I explained about the crucifixion, and how Jesus had come back to life again. All the while, the eunuch listened intently. When I paused, he waved his hand in front of his lap indicating that I should talk some more. This happened a lot, as I spoke for over two hours of all the wonders that Jesus had done in my life. He listened. I talked. The guards furnished us with more water and brought small plates of spicy food.

It was as I ate, uncertain of what it was I was eating but enjoying it nonetheless, that he spoke.

"I have been searching for truth all my life…" he laughed, and in a loud cry declared: "Today I have found it!" He beamed at me and said, "Please say a blessing over me in the name of the Jesus that you speak of."

He took my plate, still with food upon it and rested it on the side of the seat next to him, and then bowed his head.

"As I pray for you, may I place my hand upon your chest?" I asked, and then immediately felt awkward about the that suggestion as he had bosoms and I was unsure as to where to place my hand. He simply nodded, eyes still closed and waiting. I softly placed my hand right upon his chest, just under his neck, and breathed out a blessing. As I did, the weightiness of the presence of Jesus fell upon us.

"Thank you, Jesus for leading me to this man!" I declared. "I bless you now in the name of our Father who loves you. The name of the Son who gave his life for you and in the name of the Spirit who will lead you into all truth. Be blessed and may you be full of peace, in Jesus' name. Amen."

He opened his eyes, and mouthed 'amen' silently and looked around him. "But what is this sweetness, right here?" He tapped his chest twice, gently, with the fingers of his right hand, "... it feels so, so sweet and good." His face shone. "What is it?" He asked once more.

"That, my friend, is Jesus with us." I declared, and with that news he stood, awkwardly stooped over so as to not hit his head upon the fine carriage roof.

He looked radiant yet shocked in disbelief and shouted, "What! Jesus is here?"

He asked me to explain some more and while I did he held his hand to his chest, smiling.

When I explained about baptisms, he looked to the side of the dusty road. It was hard to see too far ahead as the mid-morning sun had dried up all the dew and the chariot and horses created a cloud of dust as they went. After a few minutes of looking he commanded the chariot to stop. His gaze was unnerving.

"Here's water." He simply said. "What's stopping me getting baptised right now?"

"Well, the thing is..." I bumbled. I sat with my mouth partly open trying to think what to say and thinking through lots of reasons why he couldn't: first off he was a eunuch! A man but not really one. He had one of the world's most unholy jobs. He wasn't a Jew and while I had got my head a around the fact that Samaritans could be baptised and be part of the growing church, could someone from a far distant land?

I closed my eyes because his waiting and looking at me made me feel very uncomfortable. He still held his hand upon his chest as a reminder of the presence of Jesus that had been with us. While it felt a bit awkward, the alternative reaction to not closing my eyes was to jump down from the carriage and run back the many, many miles I had travelled with him and eventually find my way home.

As I shut my eyes, I felt Jesus very near us again and I heard him speak: "Ask me, I will make the nations your inheritance, the ends of the earth your possession. This man will change an entire nation!"

I opened my eyes and asked: "Do you believe with all your heart? If you do, then I will gladly baptise you."

His white teeth shone as he beamed and through his smile he declared "I believe that Jesus is the messiah, the son of the living God!"

The water was shallow. To our knees. It was cool, flowing gently and clear. I wiggled my toes under the water and enjoyed the refreshment after the long journey and hours of talking. The gravel at the bottom of the pool twinkled and sparkled in the midday sun. We stood face to face with the guards watching above us, standing either side of the impressive carriage, looking more relaxed, and for a moment I thought I saw one hurriedly wiping a tear from the side of his face.

"Sir…" I gently said, for I still didn't know his name. "You're going to have to sit in the water, I'm afraid, it's not quite deep enough to immerse you completely if you don't." I helped him sit. "I will lean you back under the flow of the river once I declare over you what it means to be baptised."

"That's alright," he gently said. His arms were shaking.

As he sat in the river he whispered, "My name is Dawit. It means 'Beloved.' My name has never made sense to me as I have never been the beloved of anyone. Today I have become the Beloved of Jesus." He bowed his head and wept as he sat in the flow of the river. He continued, "I am in charge of the entire treasury of my Queen Kandake. She is the beautiful Queen of Ethiopia. I hope you will meet her one day, Philip, and tell her everything you have told me."

"Thank you Dawit, but I don't think I will ever meet her. I think you will be the one telling her, and many more people besides, about Jesus. Through you, my friend, an entire nation will be changed!

"Dawit, do you believe Jesus is the messiah?"

"I do, I really do!" he cried.

"Then I baptise you in his name!"

As I laid him under the flowing stream, his body created new contours for the flow of the river. His pretty face looked even more womanly. He kept his eyes open, staring straight up through the water and into mine. They almost seemed to change colour, in that moment, and become alive and fresh. Full of peace.

I lifted him up again and as he came up out of the water a triumphant cry echoed around us and the two guards also cheered and clapped their hands in celebration.

We made our way back to the carriage, only this time the two guards had jumped down and were standing waiting for us to return. One held a cloth for Dawit.

"Philip!" announced one quite sternly.

Anticipating that I may be in trouble, I stepped back towards the small river, ready to run, but the other guard had manoeuvred to block my path and was now standing behind me.

"My friend and I couldn't help overhear what you shared about Jesus and all he has done in your life."

I turned and looked at the burly guard, who was nodding enthusiastically like a little boy.

"We also want to become his followers and like our Master Dawit, can we also be baptised?"

I wasn't expecting such a question, and my first reaction was to laugh!

"Serious, guys?" I asked. They nodded and I noticed that one behind me had already begun taking off his white leather vest to place next to the sandals he'd already removed in anticipation.

"I would gladly baptise you two!" I said, but then pointed at Dawit. "But I think you two need to be baptised by the man who will bring good news to your nation!"

Dawit looked behind him as if I was pointing at someone who had mysteriously turned up to take the two baptisms. He then pointed at himself.

"Yes you, Dawit!" I laughed.

As he brought them one after the other and baptised them in a similar way to how he had been baptised, I began to feel dizzy. I was there enjoying the scene before my eyes, but felt distant at the same time. As the second guard was lifted out of the water amongst enthusiastic cheering from the three of us, I looked down at my hands, puzzled as to why there was no sound as I tried to clap enthusiastically. My hands had faded and become translucent! Then my arms, and, for a fleeting moment I looked down upon the three men, the horses and carriage and saw the shape of the river for many miles. In a matter of seconds, the scene got smaller and smaller as I was transported up and moved along, so quickly I couldn't see the land below me, and the rush of the wind was intense. What felt like two hands gripped my back, it hurt intensely, as if the hands had gripped so hard they had broken through the skin and flung me to another place.

The grass was soft beneath me and I reached behind me to rub my back. It was bruised, sore, but apart from that I was fine, strangely energised even though I couldn't quite work out how one moment I had been right next to the river and the next I was somewhere else. The sun was hot and it felt like late afternoon.

"Excuse me!" I called to a passing man leading a donkey laden with a bundle of hay that was stacked so tall that as he came to a standstill next to me the sun was blocked out from view and I sat in a shadow. "Sorry to ask such a daft question, but where am I?"

The man chuckled. "Where are you?! That is a strange question my friend! Too much of the old vino hey?!" he chuckled lifting his hand up to his lips miming someone drinking! "Where is it that you are heading?"

"Home, ideally," I said.

"Arh. That's not going to help me help you, my friend." And speaking very slowly, and somewhat loudly and as if he was talking to a child, he said:

"Now, help me to help you and tell me where it is you're heading!"

"My home is Beth Shean," I patiently said. The donkey was now grazing at the grass by my feet. The smell from the donkey seemed to attract all the flies in the neighbourhood, I wanted to finish this conversation as quickly as possible as the wave of old donkey pong kept wafting over me.

"Beth Shean!" The man erupted, "...Well if you want to head there I wouldn't start from here if I was you!"

Swishing flies from around my face I said rather impatiently, "Well, thanks for that, but where am I?"

The man got ready to continue his journey and pulled the donkey away who reluctantly started to move but managed to grab one last clump of grass.

"You're in Azotus!" chuckled the man. "Good luck getting back to Beth Shean!" he said dryly. "I hope you're not in a hurry!"

I *was* in a hurry and I did want to get back. Yet Jesus had other plans, and for five months I travelled alone, town to town, declaring the good news of Jesus. More and more people were baptised and in a land that I had thought was beyond the remit of the Messiah I saw much joy.

The five months left a trail, it was like walking in the slipstream of Jesus, seeing him go before me and work in the lives of people. Baptising Dawit was like opening a floodgate. Over five months, hundreds upon hundreds of people were baptised. It's as if his baptism had set a benchmark for who could be part of the new church or not. In my first thoughts, Dawit was so far from the kind of person I thought could be 'saved' by Jesus, but this helped me engage with everyone I met. If Dawit could be baptised and come to believe in Jesus, then everyone I met could also encounter him. Regardless of their race, religion, past or even how they looked!

Tiredness had brought me to the place where I needed to rest and get away. I had no idea that it would be for five months, and instead of resting each day I saw new churches emerge and people be baptised as I travelled from one place to another. Thankfully, word had reached Sarah that the Lord had sent me on a mission and I was seeing great revival and miracles wherever I walked until I reached Caesarea. It was there that I knew that this would become our new home and that I needed to fetch for Sarah and bring her to this place by the sea. It was magnificent, and I knew my beautiful Sarah would love our new home.

12

Our Girls

AD 43, 30 years old

The gate rattled. It wasn't a knocking, more like a good kicking.

"Sarah! Philip! Are you there?" cried an angry voice over and over as she pounded the worn red gate with her foot.

I had been snoozing in the yard. What had started off as a well-meaning prayer time ended up with me closing my eyes and then the inevitable. Four girls under six years meant I had become really good at grabbing sleep when I could. Par for the course from disturbed nights and changing nappies in the small hours.

Still groggy, I was trying to work out what the noise was all about. As I tuned in to it, I heard the unmistakable voice of Rachel who sold fish in the market. So distinctive was it, that for a moment I looked around startled, thinking I had drifted off at the busy market! We often heard her calling out what the catch of the day was and the prices of this or that. It was shrill, piercing. She had a good heart but her voice didn't match. I guess it had to be heard above the hubbub of the market – it certainly wrenched my attention from my crafty nap.

Her husband was one of the many fishermen in Caesarea. He had big, rough hands. He was good at his job and always carried around a beaming smile as if the sea gave him a deep secret of happiness. Not so with Rachel, who wore a scowl like a smacked bottom. In the midst of her shouting and kicking the gate, I heard one of the twins plead, "Let go, it really hurts!"

Sarah got there first holding the baby in her arms who was blissfully still breastfeeding and firmly suckled onto her bosom. Esther was in tow, at her heels trying to keep up with her mum as she marched, irritated by the noise of the gate and the shrieks of the fisher woman. She released the catch and the gate swung open to reveal Rachel who didn't offer a customary greeting but rather pushed the twins before their mother, still holding each one by an ear. Tears streamed down their dusty faces, but they didn't make a noise.

"Take your hands off them, Rachel." I calmly said as I walked to stand beside Sarah. At once Rachel did as I asked. The girls ran to their mum and buried their faces into her dress and carried on sobbing quietly.

"Do you want to explain what happened?" Sarah shouted.

I stood closer to her side and squeezed her hand gently. We both knew that this was a signal to calm down and so we stood simply waiting for Rachel to answer and explain why the girls had been pulled back home from the market by their ears.

We had sent them out 30 minutes previously with a shopping list of things for the evening meal. They had returned empty-handed and, as Rachel stood before us, she was clearly shaking. She wiped her hair from across her red face and tucked it into the side of her white head scarf with a trembling hand.

"Right," she spluttered. "Right. They're frightening the customers away." She placed both hands on her hips and carried on talking, way too fast, which made it hard to catch every word... "I didn't want to tell you this, you two, not after all you've done for my family and the way Matthew was healed after the accident and now that his leg is strong again, we're so grateful you know that, it's just that..." she drew breath and carried on. "Both Hermione and Eutychis started pointing and doing that thing. Again. It's freaky and I don't like it. No-one does."

Rachel now pointed at them, her eyes full of fear but brimming with tears. "We ignored it the first few times, but it's carried on week after week and to be honest Sarah, they really scare the crap out of us."

She held a hand to her mouth as if wishing the words hadn't escaped but also looking somewhat grateful that she had been able to explain how she felt. Her shoulders slumped in relief and tears dripped down her cheeks.

The gate was still open, and I indicated for her to step into the sun-filled yard as I gently closed the gate behind her, giving her a reassuring touch on her shoulder that it was all right.

She carried on, "I mean, don't get me wrong, they're such cute girls. So cute. I mean, look at that beautiful curly hair. They're adorable. But…. But…" she stammered.

I nodded, waiting for her to continue.

"When they point and proclaim that the wave is coming it puts us right off. Right off, I tell you. They've been telling us all that we will die. You have to think for a moment about how the fishermen feel about this whole thing. I mean, the whole town destroyed by the sea isn't exactly a barrel of laughs is it?"

Sarah caught my eye. We had known about the girls' vivid dreams of the sea covering our town for over a year now. They were happy children and the girls loved to play, but they also had an uncanny gift of prophecy which at times wasn't good news. Sometimes it was so accurate that people who were sceptical about the way of Jesus fell to their knees and gave their lives to him within minutes of hearing the secrets of their hearts revealed.

John, who owned one of the largest fishing boats in Caesarea, was the most recent Christian in the town and was getting baptised in a few days. We had known him for a few years and shared our faith with him regularly, even praying for his sore back which had gotten much better. But he had resolutely refused to believe in 'this Jesus mumbo jumbo' as he put it. But when out playing by the shore, the girls had asked him about his son Levi and had started to describe to John the way Levi had loved to play with stones, especially the bright orange and red ones. The girls had gathered some together and brought them to him explaining that he didn't need to fear. "It wasn't your fault you know," Hermione had declared to him. Unbeknown to everyone apart from John's wife, Levi had died over 20 years previously in an accident, drowned. He was John's only son whom he missed terribly. No-one had known about his loss, yet the twins had been told about it by Jesus.

Rachel stood waiting for a response from us.

The twins, with Esther, went to play inside, relieved that the shouting and ear-puling was over.

"We're really sorry, Rachel. We simply sent them out to get some food from the market," Sarah gently reassured and reached out a hand. Rachel took it and nodded. "Look, let us pray for you and ask the Lord to come and bring his peace to us. I can see this has upset you. I think we need to ask him about it."

She bowed her head waiting for Rachel to pray and then asked, "Can we sit down, please? I've been on my feet all day and they're killing me."

We sat and held hands, the baby now asleep on Sarah's lap. We bowed our heads and Sarah led us in prayer asking the Lord to bring his peace and that the fright that Rachel had been given by the twins would pass and that each one of us would know what the message about the wave was all about. Around us, I heard the gentle footsteps of the three girls, with a small giggle from Esther who was helping the twins with something. With our heads bowed, they had covered us as if in a tent with a large blue cotton cloth. It was Sarah's finest and had adorned our bed for many years, making the room bright and regal.

"Girls! What on earth are you doing?" I gently asked underneath the blue cloth, trying to hold back the giggles that were infectious from them.

"We are showing you what will happen Daddy!" chimed Eutychis who, with a sweet voice sung out a simple tune over and over: "The wave is coming, it will cover the town."

Rachel snapped out of the beautiful prayer and presence of God and shot up, still with the blue cloth over her head, now hanging around her like a long shawl.

She crumpled it up as quickly as she could, tearing it off her shoulders and flinging it down where we were sitting, desperately trying not to laugh. Without saying another word, Rachel nodded and looked at Sarah and me surrounded by our four girls, two of whom were still singing away their simple song. The gate creaked as she closed it behind.

Once we were sure she was out of earshot, we laughed and sang the simple song, once more placing the blue cloth like waves over us, like we were under mighty waves. It was a fun game then, but for many in the town it had really shaken them that our cute girls would pronounce something so terrible and destructive.

We didn't want or hope for destruction for our beautiful town – we loved the people that God had called us to serve and, what's more, we loved living by the beautiful sea where we would walk for miles and swim and enjoy the beauty. We had our favourite spots where we would gather and share with the growing church. One was like a cove, sheltered from the wind with soft white sand for the girls to play in. The locals had started calling that little inlet 'Baptisers Beach' due to the vast numbers of people who we had baptised over the years since we settled here, after the adventures when I had first been called by Jesus to be an evangelist.

Hiding and playing under the blue cloth, I recalled that this wasn't the first time the blue covering had had an outing.

The girls had carefully folded and placed it into the picnic basket when my mum and Judas the tanner had visited Caesarea a few months previously, visiting from Capernaum. They had been to stay for a while to get to know the new grandchildren and on one fine day Sarah and I went to walk and spend the day catching up with each other as my mum looked after the girls. She was so good with them and laughed and giggled like them, rolling and playing on the floor. It was still a miraculous sight for me seeing her so full of life and alive after spending my childhood observing my mum as just a shell of the vitality that she oozed now with our girls. It was hard to believe that she had spent twelve years without any energy, asleep most of the time.

After the picnic and while Judas and Mum looked after the baby, Esther and the twins took the blue covering out of the bag and ran up and down the beach. As they did, they carefully lifted the covering over everyone they met, young or old, and proclaimed that "the wave is coming, it will cover you like this blue cloth!" My mum reported that after she had run after them and eventually tracked them down, she had heard them answering a very upset mother on the beach who had demanded that the girls tell her who had told them about this strange message of the waves. "Jesus, the Messiah told us!" they chimed.

The wave didn't come. Well, not for many years at least.

It was always hard to imagine what the girls had declared was something that would actually happen. We began to question whether it was a literal wave they were foretelling. We had become accustomed to the wave of the gift of the Holy Spirit, but as the years rolled on and a wave didn't come, people became tired of the warning. Their message was soon lost and people forgot, especially when the girls moved away.

Who would have dreamed that the wave was caused by the seismic volcanic eruption of Mount Vesuvius on the other side of the ocean, which caused the Tsunami, which eventually *did* cover our little town of Caesarea completely? Many years after the girls had moved away and carried on their prophetic ministry and planting new churches.

The twins Hermione and Eutychis moved to Asia Minor after the death of the Apostle John and continued to work as a team, while Esther moved to join the church in Jerusalem as a teacher, using her prophetic gift to help the church grow and work out what Jesus was saying through his Spirit. Our little baby Ruth grew up so quick and joined the church in Rome soon after Sarah had died. She married a Pastor there and together they helped the church grow and spread the good news all over Europe.

We also did see waves of a metaphorical description. We saw wave upon wave of miracles. Waves of provision too, on a scale like when Jesus had fed crowds. And when the girls were all teenagers we saw wave after wave of guests who came to stay with us for rest and, often, times of profound healing.

We became known as a place of hospitality, not just our home but the whole church community. Fellow travelling missionaries as well as those of no faith would meet with God in our church. We were blessed to even host the man who had tried to kill me back in Jerusalem. Saul who had become Paul the great apostle came to stay for a time of refreshment, and the girls spent an evening prophesying over him.

But even hosting the dynamic Paul pales into insignificance compared to the elderly Roman who came and stayed with our church in Caesarea for a few days before he died. He knew that he only had a short time to live and had cried out to Jesus whom he had heard some stories about. While he slept, Jesus had met with him in a vivid dream and gave him directions to our small town, including the street name and the description of a red gate of a young church family down the road from us, a couple who had come to know Jesus one Sabbath recently as we broke bread together.

I'll always remember Justin exclaiming "this really is true!" as bread crumbs flew from his mouth around the crowded table as we gave thanks for what Jesus had done for each one of us. It was the breaking of the bread that opened the eyes of his heart and now this young couple would be used mightily by Jesus to help an old Roman soldier. The traveller had even been told by Jesus what kind of things he would expect when he came to visit. When he awoke from his dream, he wrote them down, hired a cart and horse with a driver and, after three days of travelling, he arrived at the brand new Christian couple. I will always remember that day. It was wet. For two days it had rained and the street was covered with mud. We were called from our home to come and help and trudging through the mud and dirty road meant when we arrived our lower legs were smeared yellow and brown. Thick, with mud.

The man was tall, yet stooped. Doubled over with what appeared to be abdominal pain. He was covered with a thick well-worn, lumpy brown blanket. He could hardly talk.

He sat with the blanket covering his head like an old, worn-out shepherd. The rain dripped over the top and poured over his forehead.

"I had a dream about Jesus," the man mumbled. "Am I at the right place?" His eyes darted around the covered yard, looking to see where he had eventually arrived.

"Yes, yes you have," I responded.

"Jesus told me that I would find the truth in this place. Is that right? Will you tell me how I may find forgiveness? I have been searching for the healing balm of it for most of my pitiful life."

I gently explained the gift of Jesus and how, after believing what he had done on the cross for him, he would need to welcome him into his heart and allow him to be Lord over his whole life.

By now Sarah had joined me, too caked with the mud. The young couple stood nearby holding hands and taking in the scene, ready to learn and then lead him to his room and make something for him to eat. We knelt before the old man and asked if he was ready to accept Jesus into his life, find forgiveness and be welcomed into eternal life through the free gift of his life upon the cross for his own life.

"I am ready," he gently whispered as he bent his head low. "Thank you so much for welcoming me in this place. Jesus said in my dream that I would find true freedom in this place and that His followers would love me and care for me. You have done that already beyond what words could convey. I feel so loved. Thank you."

His eyes sparkled as he smiled and he looked deeply into our eyes.

"Can we place our hands upon your head and pray for you to be made new and become a follower of Jesus right now?" Sarah confidently asked.

I had seen her lead many people into having a new start in life and it was quite natural for her to take the lead and for me to help if needed. He nodded but before Sarah was able to pray he reached up and uncovered his head from the swollen woollen sodden blanket revealing a mass of grey and white hair and a weary, battle-worn, scarred face.

We both stared at him. He, with his head bowed, weeping while Sarah and I looked at the side of his face, where an ear was missing.

Epilogue

I want to give you an opportunity to become a follower of Jesus.

My experience is that the life of Jesus is very real and his message of forgiveness and love for you and me is true.

Jesus changed my life when I was 17. I found myself at a youth event in a church hall and heard how much God loved me and that he had given Jesus to die on a cross for me. That night I chose to make him the one in charge of my life, rather than me.

Looking back, I am so pleased that I did. I had lived as if I was the most important person in the world. I didn't care for others and I used people for my own gain rather than trying to help and love people. Now, as a follower of Jesus, I long that everyone would know how much they are loved by him. Including you.

If you haven't made that decision to follow him, can I encourage you to pray from your heart and let him know what's going on in your life? I believe that Jesus longs for you to know how loved you are. I believe that Jesus brings us to God and makes us the people we were always meant to be. He is willing to take your sin upon himself and make you clean and pure.

How does he do that? Well, I believe that while each one of us has been separated from God through our sinfulness, Jesus took upon himself our sin and makes a way for us to be restored to God.

Here's an example prayer that may help you:

> *Lord Jesus, thank you for dying on the cross for me. Thank you that you rose again from death, proving that you are the one that can give new life! Thank you that you want to give me a new start.*
>
> *Please forgive me for the hurt I have caused others and help me to forgive those who have wronged me. Come to me now. Fill me with your Spirit and help me to change this world for you! Amen.*

If you don't know any Christians or of a church near you that you can check out, please visit www.christianity.org.uk

I would love to hear from you if you have made that decision to become a Christian. Please do drop me a line at chris.duffett@lightproject.org.uk or visit The Light Project Facebook page.

Become a friend of The Light Project

I hope you enjoyed this story about my hero Philip.

If you would like to become a friend of The Light Project and stand with us as we seek to send trained-up women and men to go to places that need good news, like Philip did, then please consider setting up a regular financial gift.

Our bank details are:
Sort code: 20–20–46
Account name: The Light Project
Account number: 90926914

Please do email us at office@lightproject.org.uk and we shall give you a Gift Aid form so your gift can go even further. Alternatively, you can write to us at:

The Light Project
Abbey House
Abbey Green
Chester, CH1 2JH

or contact us via our web site at
www.lightproject.org.uk